Jack

EMMA CARTER

Heartline
Books

Published by Heartline Books Limited in 2001

Copyright © Emma Carter 2001

Emma Carter has asserted her rights under the copyright,
Designs and Patents Act, 1988 to be identified as the
author of this work.

This is a work of fiction. Names and characters are the
product of the author's imagination and any resemblance
to an actual persons, living or dead, is purely coincidental.

All rights reserved. No part of this publication may be
reproduced, stored in or introduced into a retrieval system
or transmitted by any form, or by any means (electronic,
mechanical, photocopying, recording or otherwise) without
the prior written permission of the publisher. Any person
who takes any unauthorised action in relation to this
publication may be liable to criminal prosecution and
civil claims for damages.

Heartline Books Limited and Heartline Books logo are
trademarks of the publisher.

First published in the United Kingdom in 2001
by Heartline Books Limited.

Heartline Books Limited
PO Box 22598, London W8 7GB

Heartline Books Ltd. Reg No: 03986653

ISBN 1-903867-06-1

Styled by Oxford Designers & Illustrators

Printed and bound in Great Britain by
Cox & Wyman, Reading, Berkshire

EMMA CARTER

Emma Carter is a shameless romantic. A doctor, she fell in love with her husband Pete one moonless night when they were on safari in the middle of Africa. They lay for hours holding hands and gazing up at the Milky Way, which felt close enough to touch.

Ten years on, the couple live in a wooden tree-top house surrounded by bush and close to beaches, but the bedroom has a glass ceiling so that every night when they walk upstairs to bed, they can look up and see the stars without having to camp any more. Life's not all romance though: the windows leak when it rains, possums scratch at the door and tumble across their roof every night, while sulphur-crested cockatoos sometimes try to eat the house – but it is a wonderful setting for an author.

Emma says: 'Jack, in *Jack of Hearts*, is my favourite sort of hero. He's strong and powerful and very sure of himself, yet at the same time he's warm, loving and very human. I find him extraordinarily sexy. I hope you do too.'

chapter one

'So, Jack, according to the grapevine, you've hurled yourself into life at our hospital with all your usual enthusiasm.'

Jack noted the pained look. Four weeks into his new job at Wellington's Karori Hospital for Women and Children, and he'd thought that he was getting along OK. But his brother didn't look like he was making idle conversation.

'Something on your mind, Nathan?'

As Nathan straightened himself to his full six feet and folded his arms, Jack guessed that whatever was bothering him wasn't about to go away in a hurry. 'You must have known there'd be stories.'

'Stories?' He had an idea now where Nathan might be headed but he wasn't about to make it easy for him. 'You'd think people round here would be too busy running a hospital to sit around telling each other stories.'

'Come on.' Nathan's mouth compressed. 'You can't tell me you didn't realise people would talk.'

'Can't I?'

'It's a small place. Couldn't you have given that a passing thought before you seduced two midwives, and at least half a dozen nurses – not to mention the Medical Director's personal assistant?'

Jack wished he hadn't mentioned it. Robert Bingham's PA had an arresting taste for gothic dressing, but an unfortunate black widow spider seduction technique. And she'd caught him early, in his first week, before he'd understood what an offer of a tour of the hospital and this beautiful part of Wellington really meant. He hadn't been prepared. When what he'd expected to be a brief, friendly introduction to the hospital buildings and local amenities had suddenly evolved into a determined grappling match in his car, he'd been at a distinct disadvantage.

He'd escaped. Just. But he'd almost lost a shirt in the battle. '*Seduce*? Even for you, Nathan, that's kind of an old-fashioned term.'

He'd been amused at first to discover that an offer of a tour invariably included an offer to show him a whole lot more than the hospital and local suburbs. But enough was enough. After four weeks the joke had worn thin and he'd stopped accepting invitations.

'Not,' he added, 'that my social life is any of your business, *little* brother.'

He stressed the description deliberately. He was four years older than Nathan even if, at times like these, it felt as though it might be the other way round. His brother's recent marriage to the gorgeous Tessa hadn't done anything to dull Nathan's latent conservatism, Jack noted pragmatically. Nathan could always have played the field any way he wanted, but as far as Jack knew he hadn't had more than three or four relationships in his whole life. He took after their father that way. They were both steady, rock-solid types.

Jack respected that. He admired his brother.

And despite Nathan's frequently cynical observations of his lifestyle, at heart he shared Nathan's and his father's views on the sanctity of marriage vows. He knew that if he ever committed himself like that, he'd be doing it the same way as they had: sincerely, faithfully and for life.

He was open to the idea of marriage. He was thirty-five, he had a steady, permanent job now and he hoped to have kids of his own one day, so why wouldn't he be?

What he wasn't open to was any sort of compromise. Nathan would scoff, Jack knew, if he claimed openly to be a romantic. But he saw no reason to fight his basic nature. Before he asked any woman to marry him, he knew that he'd need total involvement: complete engagement of his senses, his emotions and his intellect. Physical involvement rated lower on his scale of priorities. Physical he could get anywhere.

In the meantime, until he found his ideal, life was there to be enjoyed. He wasn't about to apologise to anyone for the way he did that, least of all to Nathan.

Nathan rolled his eyes expressively but his resigned expression suggested that Jack's barb had made its point.

'You are settling in OK then?'

'I wasn't expecting any problems.' Jack had spent most of his post-graduate medical career overseas, in London, Boston and Toronto. But he was a New Zealander and he'd always intended returning, knowing that he'd made the right decision coming home when he had. His parents, while still youthful in spirit, were no longer young, and he'd been out of their lives and away for long enough. And he was enjoying his new consultant paediatrician job.

'The staff are skilled and enthusiastic and the facilities are excellent,' he commented. The hospital had only been open nine months and he was enjoying working in such modern buildings. The Children's Unit had been transferred from Wellington's main hospital to the new site and it took up just over half the floor space in the triple-storey, dual wing complex.

The only downside was the lack of a decent research facility. His office was on the first floor and he stood at the window and looked out. 'There's more than enough room to build another block,' he mused, indicating the space he meant between the building he was in now and the Obstetrics and Gynaecology complex beside it. 'A couple of labs, a good computer room and some decent office space. What do you think?'

'In your dreams.' Nathan shook his head. 'It'll never happen. There's no money.'

'No reason not to agitate.'

A flash of colour at the lower edge of the building caught Jack's eyes. His gaze shifted automatically to the blonde-haired woman in the short-skirted red suit who came skipping out of the main entrance to the opposite wing of the hospital.

He leaned forward to get a better look. As far as he could tell from above, she was gorgeous. Half joking, half not, he calculated his chances of getting down there before she disappeared. The sight of one of his fellow paediatricians following the woman out of the building, before catching her up and stopping to talk to her in what he could see was a laughing, familiar way, stopped him having to make up his mind. With any luck, he'd be able to trace her through Roger.

'Nathan? Have a look here and tell me if you know who this is.'

Nathan came across to the window. 'Roger Gleisener. I'm surprised you don't remember. He's Director of Paediatrics here. Your boss. In fact the three of us played golf two weekends ago.'

'Funny man.'

'Oh, you mean the woman?' Nathan clicked his tongue.

'Who'd have guessed? I take it you mean Kelly? What am I supposed to be looking at?'

'Kelly?' Jack's look turned sharp. *'That's* Kelly West?'

Nathan looked confused now. 'You haven't met her?'

'She's been on leave over Christmas.'

Jack studied the long legs, the gleaming hair, pleated now into a braid that reached half way down her back, and the enticing, lifting outline of her breasts beneath the close-fitting suit. His colleague hadn't been on site when he'd first come for his interview, and she'd been away from the day before Christmas Eve when he'd started work. Roger had been keen to recruit him quickly for the job in order to help cover for her absence.

'I thought she was due back tomorrow,' Jack said slowly. 'Today's she's supposed to be working in town. *That's* Kelly West…?' he repeated.

'You're surprised?'

'I wasn't expecting her to be so young.' Or sexy. Kelly was one of the two specialist children's doctors at the hospital who took a special interest in children's cancer medicine. The centre of expertise for Oncology services for the region was at Wellington's main hospital, about a twenty-five minute drive away when traffic wasn't heavy. Roger had told him that she spent several half days a week in town, including one session in her own busy private practice.

Staff at Karori talked fondly of Kelly and he'd built up a picture of a kindly, matronly, pleasant middle-aged woman with a family of her own.

The vision below, laughing and waving her arms around at Roger, was vibrant with energy and more bombshell than matron. 'Married?'

Nathan made a derisive sound. 'Would it make any

difference?' Jack sent him a hard look and his brother had the grace to look shamefaced. 'OK, OK,' he muttered. 'Divorced.'

'She doesn't look old enough.'

'Some guy years ago. Before she worked here. Nobody knows anything about him.'

'Children?'

'Nope.' Nathan's bleep flared and he pressed the button to check the illuminated number, then moved to Jack's desk and his phone.

Jack, preoccupied watching his colleagues below, didn't tune into his brother's conversation and when Nathan said, 'I have to go. It's Delivery Suite,' he barely registered the words. When Kelly and Roger disappeared beneath him into the shadow of the building and he looked around, he was surprised to find his brother gone.

The wards were busy the rest of the day and his afternoon clinic was full, so it was after seven before he was free to leave. He'd been on call since Saturday morning, putting his hours on call and on duty up to about eighty in a row. And he'd been up all Sunday night in the Intensive Care Unit with a child who'd been admitted with an infection related to meningitis. He still needed a couple of hours in his office to catch up on paperwork, but he was tired and thirsty and if he had any hope of getting through the work, he needed caffeine.

The doctor's common room, upstairs on the top floor of the same wing, was empty but the television blared out regardless. He turned off the noise, boiled water, spooned grey hospital-issue coffee granules into a paper cup and added the water. He lifted the cup towards his mouth, but before it reached his lips the door was flung open and there was the noise of someone rushing in.

He swung around and smiled.

Kelly West took a couple of steps into the room, looked at him and stopped short, her expression startled. 'Oh!' she exclaimed. 'It's Lover Boy!'

He stared at her, momentarily lost for speech, and she laughed.

'At last,' she went on, clearly unabashed by the strangeness of her greeting. 'What luck! I was hoping I'd find time to catch up with you today, but I've been stuck in town at meetings and clinics and I thought you'd have left already. Kelly West.' She lifted one foot, slid off a very high, red heel, and hobbled over to him, shoe in hand, her other arm extended.

'Welcome to Karori, Dr McEwan,' she continued. 'Good to meet you finally. How are you settling in?'

'It's Jack. And well. I've settled in fine.' Jack shook the hand she'd held out then kept hold of it. Close up he saw she wasn't as young as the youthfulness of her figure had implied earlier, but her skin was soft-looking and creamy, her sapphire eyes sparkled up at him warmly and her mouth formed a perfect, red welcoming bow.

Her smile was so catchy, he smiled right back. He considered never letting go of her hand. *'Lover Boy?'*

'Sorry.' But her laugh was light and serene and as appealing as it was unrepentant. 'Your reputation precedes you.'

Catching him off guard, she jerked her fingers out of his grip, and her eyes gleamed mischievous acknowledgement that they both knew he'd held her hand far too long for politeness.

'You'd think people round here would too busy running a hospital to sit around engaging in idle gossip.'

'Oh, come on!' She laughed again. 'It's a small place.

If you're going to race around ravishing nurses left right and centre, you've got to expect to cause a little stir. And getting caught in a black Porsche in the car park on your first week in the job, making out with the Medical Director's personal assistant, probably wasn't the smartest move you could have made. Not if you wanted to maintain a low profile.'

'We weren't,' he said wearily, 'making out.' Was that afternoon going to haunt him for ever?

'Tell it to the judge. Or maybe just to the two student nurses, the midwife and the elderly technician from the pathology department who got the best view, apparently, so he's said to be the most credible witness. He is also, by the way, apparently still reeling from the shock.'

'How elderly? Elderly enough to need new glasses?'

'It's a long shot,' she said lightly. 'But maybe I'll give you the benefit of the doubt.' She lifted a shapely calf and shed her second shoe as well, taking an instant seven or so centimetres off her height. 'Still, even if your prowess has been exaggerated...' The way her eyes narrowed suggested that she doubted it. 'You've certainly still livened things up around here. Is that coffee I smell?'

'Of a sort.' His own had gone cold. 'I'll boil more water. Black?'

'And strong, please,' she called back, smiling at him over her shoulder as she headed towards the bank of lockers along the side wall of the room. 'Thanks. You're an angel. And please forgive and forget the bimbo suit.' She swung an arm to indicate the fire-engine-red suit, along with the heels she'd now thrown on to a chair, before twiddling a combination lock to open one of the grey, metal doors.

'I'm a jeans and shirt and jersey girl normally,' she

added. 'But I had a big funding meeting this morning with the dear Dr Bingham in administration, and I find things go better around Bobby if I flash a bit of leg.'

Jack could understand that. He even felt a little sympathy for the man, who'd probably started out with fine intentions of trying to keep down his budget. 'Sugar?'

'No thanks. Sweet enough already, and all that.' She was behind her locker door, undressing briskly, and although he'd turned to ask about the sugar, rather than deliberately to catch her – it hadn't occurred to him she could be changing – the metal door was narrow enough to offer him a pleasant view.

He admired the long, curving thighs and the enticing outline of her bottom beneath the cream, high-cut briefs she wore and settled back against the counter to enjoy the show. 'Coffee's ready,' he pointed out, considering it only fair to give her some token reminder of his presence.

'Be there in a tick.'

Still turned away, she wiggled a pair of faded jeans up over her thighs and bottom, swiftly zipped and buttoned, then shed her jacket to reveal a smooth, pale back and midriff and a low cut cream bra. She wasn't self-conscious, he noted. With natural, graceful movements, she hauled on a green sweater and hung her suit away in the locker. She thrust her feet into a pair of flat, black shoes, lifted her braid away from under her jersey and let it drop down her back, then smoothed the garment down over her hips, took a brisk step back and closed and locked the metal door, before turning confidently towards him.

He saw her falter when she realised that he'd been watching her, but the hesitation was eye-blinkingly brief, and her smile was back, as broad as ever, before he could even be sure it had faded.

'Coffee. Mmm...' She came towards the drink he'd held out as a silent offering. 'Boy, do I need caffeine.' She took the paper cup and swallowed an appreciative mouthful as she stepped back. 'Sorry about the striptease.'

She sounded breathless, and the blue eyes that had earlier regarded him so boldly, interestingly now started dipping and diving as if intent on avoiding his. 'I live in Wadestown,' she added. 'It's not that far away, I know. But I'm on call tonight, and since I've been stuck in town all day I'd feel bad about arriving late just because I went home to change on the way. It had to be a case of either getting rid of the suit now – or putting up with being stuck in it all evening.'

She smoothed herself again with her free hand, drawing his attention back to the enticing curve of her hip and thigh beneath her jeans. Although she'd done nothing to wrinkle herself in the meantime, she repeated the gesture a few seconds later. 'So, you're settling in all right I take it?'

'Getting used to the place,' Jack acknowledged. She'd already asked him that, he registered, speculating, as she walked away from him, on the intriguing prospect that Kelly West might not be quite as breezily sure of herself as she seemed intent on pretending.

He wondered if he was making her nervous.

She walked towards the bank of armchairs in front of the room's television set and his eyes lowered automatically. She moved beautifully, he noticed again. He contemplated how she might move in bed and the vision upped his blood pressure a notch. 'You'll have to remind me where Wadestown is.'

'Oh, just down the hill into town, then back up to the left.' She took the end seat then swivelled around towards him. She swung her long legs gracefully over the arm of the chair, then eyed him over her coffee. 'Sorry, I forgot you wouldn't know Wellington. It's an easy drive, not far at all really. The flat's small and a bit chilly in winter, but I love the area and the rent is a bargain. It's ideal for working here because it only takes me ten minutes to drive up if I'm needed for an emergency overnight. I hear you're living in staff accommodation,' she added. 'How are you finding it?'

'Comfortable.' Jack tilted his head. 'Surprisingly so, for hospital accommodation.' The townhouse was fully furnished and modern and less than five minutes' walk from the wards. 'I'll get around to buying in the area at some stage.'

Looking up at him the way she was, the light from the high windows above turned her eyes to dark smudges in her face. He walked across and took the chair opposite her, to change the angle so he could see her properly. He noticed that the red of her nail polish matched the suit she'd been wearing. She'd gone to a lot of effort for her meeting. He wondered if she'd been given everything she wanted by Robert Bingham, and decided that she probably had. If she hadn't, then the man was made of far stronger stuff than he was.

When it came down to political gamesmanship with administration, he acknowledged that they had an obligation to their patients to use every weapon available. But he was still surprised that she'd deliberately used her looks. Her pragmatism interested him. If he believed everything he'd heard about Kelly, then she was clearly a dedicated, devoted, hard-working and highly intelligent physician. In his experience, women doctors who'd had to fight their way up through invisible barriers to achieve positions of power – despite the majority of medical students now being female, the higher echelons of medicine in New Zealand remained male-dominated – would slit their throats before stooping to using sex to achieve their ends.

'How long have you been in Wellington?' he asked.

'Almost four years.' She hadn't touched her coffee for a few minutes and now she looked down at it. 'I grew up in Auckland and I trained there. This is my first job away from the city and my first consultant position.'

She lifted her fair head again and her braid swung over the edge of her chair in a long, silken rope. He studied it. He pictured himself as a mythical prince slowly climbing it, and he imagined the joy of finding her at the top. The imagery and his experience of it startled him. It was corny, and clichéd and he didn't normally find himself considering fairy-tales.

'Is it too soon for you to say if you're here to stay yet?'

'To stay?'

'After your interview, Roger Gleisener admitted he was worried that with your qualifications and experience you might decide to return to England, or North America eventually.'

That puzzled him. He hadn't realised the head of children's medicine had doubted his commitment to Karori. 'My contract's for three years.' Consultant paediatrician jobs in New Zealand's main teaching hospitals came up only rarely and he wouldn't be throwing this one away. 'If I'm offered the chance to stay longer I intend taking it.'

'Of course you'll be offered it.' Now Kelly looked puzzled. 'Getting you down here was a huge coup for Roger. We were half expecting The Starship to pull a swifty and hold on to you at the last minute.'

On his return to New Zealand he'd locumed briefly at

The Starship, Auckland's main children's hospital, covering for a paediatrician who'd taken research leave. The other hospital *had* offered him a permanent position before he'd left, but by then he'd been committed to Karori. 'That was only a three month fill-in job.'

'Before your interview, Roger showed me your résumé. We were very impressed.' She smiled a little ruefully. 'No, more like incredibly impressed. Boston. Toronto. Great Ormond Street. You've worked at places the rest of us only read about. We both thought, Wow! Is there really a chance we can get this guy? Although, of course, in comparison you make us look like a bunch of hicks.'

'There's nothing remotely hick-like about you, Dr West,' he observed smoothly, earning himself a sharp, sideways flickered look. 'And Roger's one of the finest paediatricians in the country.'

'Big fishes, small pond.'

There was an edge to the words and his eyes narrowed interestedly. Had something – her marriage perhaps? – stopped her furthering her career by working abroad when she might have wanted to? 'You haven't travelled?'

'Never. Not even as tourist. I've never been out of New Zealand.'

'But you've been away four weeks.'

'Only visiting my mum and my sister and her family.' The crisp way she cut off the words suggested she wasn't keen on further questioning. 'Well, that and work. It wasn't a real holiday in the "holiday-holiday" sense. I stayed with Mum in Auckland over Christmas while I locumed for a friend, who needed a month away from her practice to have a baby. It was very quiet. Unlike you, I've never been adventurous. I dislike going outside my comfort zone. I'm afraid I'm a plain, boring, old-fashioned homebody at heart.'

Jack pondered the incongruity of that. Why, he wondered, would a woman who looked and acted so thoroughly modern, who seemed confident and aware of her sexuality and who could – almost – calmly undress in front of a strange man, talk about herself in such dismissive terms?

She tipped her head back to reveal a long, creamy throat, finished her coffee in two quick swallows, crushed the cup in her hand and swung her legs around. 'Still,' she added briskly, 'you can see the world on computers these days. No need to risk life and limb by visiting the great sights in person any more. I'd better get myself off to the wards. I told Spencer I'd go round at seven so he's probably swearing his head off about me keeping him waiting by now. Any one I should know about?'

'Cindy Bunker, an eight-year-old in Intensive Care,' Jack told her thoughtfully. 'The unit knows to call me directly for any problems overnight. I'll review her again in an hour or so and Spencer knows all about her.' Doctor Spencer Turnball was the registrar who worked for both of them.

'I'll get him to brief me,' Kelly said with a nod. She dumped her crumpled cup into the bin close to him. 'Nothing else?'

'No one you should be called to.' Cindy was his only major concern, and he'd be keeping a close eye on her himself. His other patients were either steady or improving and he didn't expect any changes before he was back on duty in the morning.

'I need you to update me on any of my patients you've seen this month. How about if we meet before the ward round in the morning?'

'Sure.' He already knew that he'd be prepared to meet her any time, anywhere she wanted. 'Seven?'

'Perfect.' She made for the door. 'Thanks. I appreciate you coming in that early. I'm looking forward to working with you,' she added, turning to smile at him. 'The nurses tell me you've done a spectacular job while I've been away.' She smiled at him again as she pulled the door open. 'I can't wait to see you in action.'

Jack was looking forward to seeing Kelly in action too, he reflected. He was looking forward to that very much.

chapter two

Kelly was waiting in the common room, coffees poured, when Jack arrived a few minutes before seven o'clock the next morning. He wore cream chinos and an olive polo-style shirt and he looked tall, strong and rugged – and completely and absolutely too appealing for her peace of mind.

Jack McEwan had the sort of shoulders, she registered, that made a woman's thoughts turn to how it might feel to grip on to them.

Other women's thoughts, she told herself firmly. Not hers. No, thank you very much! And she was breathing more quickly than normal because she'd been hurrying. That was all.

Given all the gossip flying around about him, she'd expected him to be spectacularly good looking, model-like even, and she'd been surprised the night before to find him not pretty or smooth, but instead a real man; hard-looking and powerfully masculine. His skin was rough textured, as if he'd spent a lot of time outdoors and his nose looked as if it'd been broken once or twice. Rugby, she assumed. Either that or fighting. He looked equally capable of excelling at both.

But his eyes, now they really *were* spectacular. She'd never seen that particular green-yellow, almost tea-like colour before. What she especially liked was the amusement she saw in them. It was an amusement that suggested he'd decided that life wasn't meant to be taken too seriously; that there was adventure to be had and he wanted it.

The adventure bit left her cold. It even frightened her. But since it felt like a very long time since she'd been in a position to take life anything but seriously, she understood why his devil-may-care look might appeal to her.

But it didn't mean she liked the feeling.

Kelly, she told herself sternly, get a grip!

He was carrying a stack of notes and a file of letters, and he dumped both on to the table between them. His forearm, when he sat beside her, made hers look sickly white and scrawny in comparison, and she studied the contrast silently, until her eyes found the thick silver watch at his wrist and she registered the brand name.

She averted her gaze sharply. She didn't begrudge him his wealth, of course, but even now she still found it hard to remember just how easily money could disappear, and her ex-husband had shared Jack's taste for expensive consumer goods. Warwick had enjoyed his watches. But she was the one paying for them now, she reflected wearily. The bitterness she'd once felt about the mountain of debt her ex-husband had saddled her with had long ago faded to resignation, but still, every now and then, reminders prickled.

They worked through the list of children Jack had seen for her while she'd been away. With impressive brevity, he outlined the results of new investigations or changes he'd made to their treatment. He was organised and efficient and his summaries were fluid and succinct. And even though she found herself more distracted than she wanted to be by his physical presence, the task was accomplished relatively quickly.

'I met someone else you probably remember.' This

after they'd finished when he went to fetch them refills of the hospital's disgusting coffee. 'A seven-year-old called Tammy Forest. She said to say a big hello to you.'

'Tammy?' Tammy had been referred to Kelly with acute leukaemia. She'd given her six months of chemo and she'd been in full remission for a total of twenty months, but there was a long way to go before she'd be able to consider her cured.

She pushed back her chair and followed him towards the sink area. 'She should have been sent directly to me today or into town until now, you shouldn't have been asked to see her,' she said apologetically.

After the session they'd just had, with his level of experience and after hearing reports on how well he'd performed while she was away, she had absolute faith in Jack's diagnostic skills. But she worked in a highly specialised field. In her absence, her young cancer patients were supposed to have been referred to one of her colleagues in Wellington. 'What's happened?'

'Nothing to Tammy.' He looked around from where he was making the drinks. 'She's fine. The family's GP referred her brother for advice on his asthma. He's going to be coming to chest clinic until we get things under control. Knowing his family history, I checked him out carefully and there's no other problem with him. His sister was disappointed I didn't have a kiwi on my stethoscope.'

Kelly let out her breath slowly, relieved. As Tammy's brother, Jack's patient had a higher risk than normal of developing leukaemia, but clearly that wasn't the case here. She retrieved her stethoscope from around her neck and showed him the miniature, furry Kiwi bird she kept clipped to the tubing. 'It squeaks,' she told him, squeezing it to demonstrate. 'I've never heard one in real life but I'm told that's not authentic. Still fun though. Kids love it.'

'You've never heard a kiwi?' He took the furry bird from her, leaning back against the cupboards and studied it. 'What sort of New Zealander do you call yourself, woman?'

She tilted her chin, a touch defensive. 'One who's never been interested in getting wet, muddy and scared traipsing through the bush in the middle of the night searching for rare birds.'

'No true New Zealander should be too busy to go in search of a kiwi,' he decreed sternly. 'What about when you were a kid? You said last night that you're an Auckland girl. Didn't your Mum and Dad take you camping up north in the kauri forests? There were kiwis all over the place up there when we were young. You might have heard them at night, just not recognised the call.'

'My family wasn't the camping sort.' She reached out and retrieved the bird from his grip, unhappily aware that her fingers started tingling immediately they brushed his.

They hadn't been the holidaying sort of family, full stop. A year after her father died, the family GP told her mother to take a break away. Ever obedient, her mother joined a group of women from her church for a short cruise to Fiji. But she didn't enjoy the experience and these days she rarely left her Auckland suburb. During the month Kelly had just spent with her, she'd managed to coax her mother out to tea twice and out once to a show, but she doubted she'd keep up the activities now that she was alone again. Her mother was used to a quiet life confined to church, a weekly shopping trip, and tea on a Monday night with Kelly's younger sister and family who lived one street away. She rarely ventured far from home.

'Apart from when I was a baby, I've never been north

of Albany,' she admitted gingerly. Albany was only just north of Auckland. Now it was part of the city's suburban sprawl, but when she'd been young it had been untouched countryside. 'I haven't even made it to South Island yet, even though we're so close here.'

He shook his head. 'I'm shocked. That's beautiful country down there. It's part of your heritage. You should see it.'

'I told you that I wasn't a traveller.' It wasn't a sin but still she felt embarrassed. 'I hate flying and I'm sure I'd be sick on the ferries. But I will try and brave it out one day. I'd love to see Mount Cook and the lakes. And Fiordland, of course,' she mused. She had a calendar showing Mitre Peak on her fridge. 'It looks beautiful in pictures.'

'You could see a lot in a long weekend. You could fly to Queenstown and hire a car. It'd be fun.'

'Maybe.' But even if she had the time, a trip like that would be expensive. 'I work most weekends. When I'm not on call here I cover a private emergency clinic in Wellington. And I do an extra night or two in general practice. I don't have a lot of free time.'

'Doesn't sound like you have any.' He eyed her curiously. 'Is getting rich that important to you?'

Only someone who'd never had to think about money would have asked such a question. She remembered the watch. And the top-of-the-line Porsche. 'It would help,' she said blandly, meeting his speculative green-yellow look neutrally.

She knew she should leave. She had no intention of discussing her private life and her finances with him. Yet she found herself reluctant to take the first step and that disturbed her.

Being around Jack McEwan could get addictive, she

acknowledged. The combination of uncompromising masculinity, sexual confidence and a sharp intellect was a powerfully seductive combination.

'It all helps,' she repeated. She gathered up the files they'd finished with and tried to collect her senses and her head. 'Shall I meet you on the ward in half an hour?'

He drained his coffee. 'I'll join you now.'

That wasn't what she'd wanted, but still she could hardly protest when he dropped his own cup into the bin and followed her to the ward.

She saw, on the round, that he was superb with children. The nurses had told her that already, but when she saw him working she understood what they'd meant. Paediatricians had to be able to establish rapport with children. Without the ability to draw out a child and inspire confidence, a clinician wouldn't be able to work effectively. But Jack was better than effective.

'Enough fussiness,' he decreed, when one of his little patients, Brett Spinks, an eight-year-old with a freckle-covered, normally cheeky but now moody face, pushed away the meal being delivered for him as they arrived. He reached for the remote for Brett's television and VCR and muted the loud cartoon he was watching. 'Time we force-fed you an eel or two.'

'Eels?' The child brightened fractionally and he sat up. '*Eels?*'

'Fat, juicy, slippery eels,' Jack said carelessly. He crouched and examined Brett's tummy. 'All munched up in a slimy sandwich. Fresh from the creek at the back of the hospital. They're great. You'll love them, won't he, Dr Kelly?'

'Only if he likes them really, *really* slimy,' Kelly warned.

Brett looked intrigued. 'They might electrify me.'

Jack grinned. 'Not if you wear rubber shoes when you eat them.' He lifted his stethoscope from around his neck and listened to Brett's chest. 'What you definitely need,' he told him, 'is a double dose of eel sandwich.'

'If I eat them, will you let me sit in your car?'

'No eels in the car,' Jack decreed. 'They'll get loose and hide under the seats. I'll never find them again and they'll stink.'

'Can I just touch your car then?'

'I don't think so.' Jack shook his head. 'No, mate. Sorry. Nothing personal, Brett, but I don't want your grubby fingerprints all over it. And if I let you, I'd have to let all the kids. It'd be a never-ending nightmare. It costs me too much in cleaning bills as it is.'

Brett pursed his mouth. 'What if I eat the eels, wash my hands, and then promise to wash your car afterwards? Can I touch it then?'

'I'll do you a deal.' Jack crouched again. 'I'll do you the best deal of your life. You eat this,' he said, swinging the tray with Brett's meal back across the child's bed. 'And if you save me the job of having to go down to the creek to fish out your eels, and if you eat everything put in front of you until you're better, *and* you wash your hands ten times and promise not to touch anything – then the day you're ready to go home, I'll let you sit in my car. Ten seconds. No longer. And remember, no touching anything. And you have to keep it secret. I don't want any other kid hearing about this.'

'Ten seconds. Wow!' Brett seemed impressed. 'OK. Can my Dad be there too?'

'Don't push it,' Jack advised, punching the child's arm playfully as he rose to his feet. 'Eat your tea.'

'I'm going to,' Brett vowed solemnly. 'When can I go home?'

'Sunday, if your X-ray's good.'

Kelly smiled up at him as they left Brett's side room. Brett suffered from chronic kidney failure, and he needed dialysis every other day while he waited for a suitable transplant organ to become available. He was in hospital now because of a chest infection.

'How did he sound?' she asked.

'Big improvement.' Jack's arm brushed her sleeve when he paused to write a summary in Brett's notes. The contact was so light she barely felt it, yet her skin heated immediately.

'Are you really going to let him sit in your car?'

'As long as he sticks to the rules.'

'You're possessive with your toys.'

'Not all of them.' He slanted her a sideways look from close up. 'Why? Want to play?'

'No, thank you.' It came out sounding prim, and Kelly felt the flush that had started at her arm extend up to her chest. 'Is it true what they say about men and their cars?'

'Probably.' He didn't look up again, but after they'd finished the round and returned to the main nursing station to look through the children's X-rays, he said, 'Remind me – exactly what *is* the connection between men and cars?'

'Oh, you know.' Kelly looked up at the film they were studying and laughed. She liked him, she realised. She hadn't entirely expected to. She hadn't even wanted to, at least not without reservations. She'd once been married to a man who went through women at what she guessed was roughly the same rate as Jack did, so she knew how damaging he could be. Plus she had the added problem of the disruptive effect he seemed to be having on her senses. But she did. She did like him. And she liked, very much, the way he was with the children. Her natural approach, particularly to her sickest charges, tended to be gentle and soothing, and that worked in its own way. But he treated them with a casual, lazy amusement, and they responded playfully in return.

She admired his open warmth and the lack of self-consciousness in him. In her experience the first attribute, particularly, wasn't common in men. 'They say men who drive expensive cars are compensating for sexual inadequacies.'

'Oh, I'm sure that's true.' He smiled. 'Never date a man with a Ferrari, you'll be disappointed. This film's better than yesterday. I'll change his antibiotics over to oral. What do you drive?'

'Let's just say it's currently valued by my insurance company at around three thousand dollars. And if it's ever stolen or written-off, I won't be too upset.'

He raised a quizzical eyebrow.

'Frankly, I reckon the insurance company are kidding themselves,' she told him. 'The only offer I've ever had for my car was for less than half that amount.' She'd been driving the same small car for four-and-a-half years and she was its sixth owner. 'Which I'd guess,' she added dryly, 'is around a hundred times less than yours is worth. Tell me, am I even close to being right? Or is it more like two hundred times?'

He grinned. 'I never keep track. Have you considered upgrading your car?'

In my dreams, she thought wryly. 'It's very reliable.'

'Ah, but is it exciting? Is it fun to drive? Does it make your breathing speed up and your heart race?'

'Reliability,' she said firmly, 'is all that matters to me. I'm very happy living without the rest.'

He laughed. 'Well you know what that just tells me, Kelly West,' he filed the X-ray back into its folder. 'It tells me that you haven't truly tried the rest.'

'I have to go. My clinic's enormous this morning and I want an early start,' she told him firmly.

Even if she hadn't been busy, Kelly knew that she'd have been forced to come up with some excuse. Because those gorgeous, knowing green eyes of his were far, *far* too perceptive.

chapter three

Directly after her morning clinic, Kelly met Sarah Bingham and Margie Lomax for lunch in the canteen.

The meeting was a regular thing for Tuesdays. Sarah was married to Robert Bingham, the hospital's medical director, and now that the youngest of her three children had started school she'd begun working three days a week as a medical officer in the Gynaecology department. Margie was a consultant paediatrician and she worked closely alongside her own husband, the Intensive Care Unit director, Ben Lomax.

All three of them were on the executive committee for the new Karori branch of their local Medical Women's Association, and part of the reason for the meeting was to discuss issues related to that. But over the years she'd been in Wellington, Kelly had grown close to both women and the sessions were far more social than business.

They took their regular table by the window, from where they had views over the houses alongside the hospital and up to the dry, bush-scarred hills beyond. Kelly smiled apologetically at Sarah as she sat down.

'Did Bobby tell you I flashed my legs at him again yesterday?'

'He told me that he'd decided to try to push your funding through with the board,' Sarah revealed dryly. Kelly was relieved to see she was smiling. 'Last week he told Roger Gleisener there was no way any project would be getting more clinical trial money this year. So I reckoned you must have pulled something really underhand.'

'A short skirt and pictures of some of our most beautiful babies,' Kelly admitted. 'I decided it was worth a try. The legs worked when we wanted the extra beds opened last winter. This time I suspect it was the baby photos that did it.'

'As if.' Sarah rolled her eyes. 'Bobby goes weak at the knees at the sight of a decent leg.' She held out her own strikingly spectacular pair. 'Sometimes I think these are the only reason he married me. Eleven years this month and he still can't keep his hands off them.'

Now Margie rolled her eyes. 'Sarah, you know he told us he married you for your organisational skills,' she chided.

Sarah laughed. 'Just like Ben married you for your dress sense,' she countered.

When Kelly looked up from her sandwich, puzzled by Margie's shocked yelp, Sarah waved a hand at her. 'Back in Wellington, before Margie and Ben started going out, Margie used to wear this transparent pink blouse to work,' she confided. 'Ben was so jealous about other guys looking at her, that he married Margie so he could veto her wardrobe.'

'It wasn't transparent,' Margie protested, laughing now. 'It was an ordinary blouse. A plain, pink blouse. I didn't know that there was anything wrong with it, and I still don't. You know, it was only when I stood against a window that you could see...'

'Enough said!' Sarah nodded triumphantly. 'You see, Kelly? I told you. She might look prissy, but in reality she's a loose woman. The day they married, I bet Ben chucked that blouse straight in the bin.'

'Well you'd be wrong,' Margie came back swiftly.

'Ah!' Sarah smiled knowingly. 'He gets private shows now, does he? Don't say any more, we get the picture!'

Kelly joined in the laughter. Despite her own disastrous experience of marriage, she was pleased her friends were happy and fulfilled in their own partnerships. Robert Bingham might have an eye for legs, but he'd never once tried to flirt even innocently with her. And if anyone needed proof that he worshipped Sarah and the children, they only had to look at the dozen or more photographs of them which he kept around his walls and on his desk. And Ben and Margie were more in love than any other couple she knew, and their two children were beautiful.

'Now, Kelly, what about you?' Sarah asked once the laughing settled. 'Let's hear all about him.'

Kelly smiled. 'All about who?'

'Your new consultant.' Sarah started in on her bran muffin. 'Stop taunting us, you fiend. The delectable Dr McEwan. There's been loads of gossip. What's your opinion?'

Kelly felt her colour flutter. 'He seems nice.' She picked up her chicken and avocado sandwich but didn't take a bite. 'I've been away all month, don't forget. We met last night for ten minutes then we did a ward round together this morning. We talked.' She strove to sound casual. 'He's great with the kids. He seems OK.'

'*OK*...?' Sarah looked at her sideways. '*Nice*...?' Pull the other one, Kelly!'

'What?' Kelly groaned inwardly. She guessed from her friends' sceptical expressions that she maybe hadn't sounded quite as off-hand as she'd intended. '*What*?'

'He's not just OK, you ninny.' Even Margie seemed bemused. 'He's extremely sexy.'

'How would you know?' She was startled. She agreed, of course she agreed. But while she might have expected the observation from Sarah, Margie was normally far more reserved. 'Since when have you looked at any man but Ben?'

'Since Jack McEwan tried to pick me up at the golf club, three weeks ago.' Obviously enjoying their stunned reaction to that bombshell, Margie laughed at them. 'I thought he was very charming. If I wasn't a happily married woman, I'd have been tempted.'

Both Kelly's and Sarah's mouths had dropped right open. 'What?' Sarah gasped. 'You're kidding. What happened?'

'Nothing *happened*.' Margie smiled. 'I was sitting on my own and he came over and smiled and introduced himself. We talked for a while and he offered to buy me a drink. I said thank you, but by the time he came back from the bar, Ben had arrived and Jack realised who I was – and that was that. I've seen him often since and he's always charming, but there's nothing else. Clearly married women don't do it for him.'

'More likely he knows Ben would kill him,' Kelly argued.

'Oh, I think they'd be pretty evenly matched.' Margie sipped her tea. 'So if you say you're not even a tiny bit interested, Kelly, you know we won't believe you.'

'I didn't say I wasn't curious,' Kelly admitted. Naturally she was. She'd been intrigued for three weeks, ever since the day she'd rung from Auckland to get a briefing on her patients, and had instead been regaled with tales of the hospital's new consultant. Who wouldn't be curious with those sorts of stories going around?

But close up he was unsettling. His appreciation was

far too warm, too frank, and too open. Even thinking about the way he'd looked at her the night before, when she'd turned around after changing out of her suit – it had never occurred to her that he'd be able to see anything behind the locker – made her colour rise. Kelly suddenly realised that she'd probably blushed more in the past eighteen hours since meeting him, than she had in the whole of the last decade. For some unknown reason, Jack McEwan made her feel extraordinarily nervous.

Yet like most women, she supposed, she was used to being looked at by men. When she was younger the attention had made her self-conscious, but she barely registered it these days. On the few occasions when she did, she'd perfected the art of breezy deflection. Men were like background wallpaper in her life. They were there all around her, inescapable, every day, but she rarely allowed them to make any impression on her.

It worried her that Jack had got through her defences so easily. And it doubly worried her that he hadn't politely turned away when she'd changed her clothes. 'He's no gentleman,' she declared.

Sarah burst out laughing. 'Kelly, you're priceless. You're the opposite of Margie. On top you're all sexy and sassy and confident, but scratch the veneer and underneath you're like a prim little nun. I'm not saying marry the man and bear his children. Not that it wouldn't be fine too,' she added quickly, 'if you were interested. But from the little you've said over the last couple of years, I don't get the impression you're looking for that. For now, I'm saying that you deserve some fun. Get rid of some tension. With your looks, you'd pull him with no trouble. Why not fool around a little?'

Kelly blinked. 'What, have an affair with him?'

'It's great idea.' Sarah shrugged. 'Don't look at me like that, you prude. It's the twenty-first century. You're free as a bird, and even if you insist on working so much you never go out, surely you could still scrape together a spare hour or two to see if he lives up to his reputation. It'd be fun. Providing you take precautions, of course, but who wouldn't these days? The last time you let me set you up in a date was with that computer guy, and that has to be a year and a half ago at least. And I know for a fact that you sent him away with a flea in his ear so you didn't get anything that night. It's probably been ages for you, hasn't it?'

'Who's counting?' Kelly answered quickly. She wasn't. She definitely wasn't. But it was almost four years since her divorce. She knew that much without having to think about it, because her birthday was coming up and – a painful coincidence – the dates were the same. She'd been out with men occasionally since she'd lived in Wellington, of course. But they'd all been blind dates set up by well-meaning friends like Sarah, and every one had been a disaster. Tedious evenings of stilted conversations, ending with her having to fight off the eager advances of men who seemed to assume she had to be desperate for sex, hadn't left her with an urge to go any further down that track.

She wasn't dead physically. Until things had gone sour with her marriage, sex had been an enjoyable facet of her life and she did miss it. She even still had the occasional erotic dream. She'd had one last night. But while the thought of the actual physical act of making love with an attractive man like Jack McEwan wasn't repugnant to her, there was no way in the world she was in any position to cope with a relationship right now.

The scars from her marriage had healed, she thought. She was no longer hurt or angry and her self-esteem was intact again, but she was still wary. And this year work had to be her priority.

For the first time since before her divorce, Kelly felt as if she was at last within sight of her goal. By keeping her spending as low as she could this year, and by working harder than she'd ever worked in her life, there was a chance that she just might, finally, be able to pay off the last of the money she owed. That would make her, at last, free of debt. She was so close to that freedom now she could almost taste it.

In just one more year she'd be able to have some choice again in her life. She'd be able to make decisions, even simple ones like which brand of bread she preferred, based on what she wanted and not on cost. She'd be able to afford to visit her mother and her sister and her nieces more than once a year, and she'd be able to pay for her mother to come down and stay with her. She wouldn't have to worry any more about her mother getting sick, or even worry about getting sick herself and not being able to afford the bills and the time off work.

She might even, perhaps in about two years, be able to afford a deposit on a house of her own so she'd feel as if she was putting down roots again at last, and really belonging somewhere.

The vision was heady.

In the meantime, though, she definitely did *not* need some man hanging around, distracting her from her work, forcing her to spend money on trying to look nice and demanding her attention.

'The best thing about men like Jack McEwan...' Sarah mused. 'Or, at least, wildly promiscuous men in general, is the fantasy they allow us that it might be possible to have great, steamy, no-strings sex with a man without ever feeling guilty about it. A man whose primary focus is sex isn't going to object if a woman tells him all she wants is a one- or two-night stand. In a lot of ways, it'd be liberating, don't you think, to be able to treat a man casually without worrying about the emotional baggage we normally all carry around with us?'

Kelly had looked up sharply as soon as Sarah had said the bit about no-guilt sex. 'Wouldn't you consider it immoral to go out with a man, purely because you want him physically?'

'I agree it's immoral to deceive someone in order to get sex,' Sarah answered smartly. 'But I don't think it's immoral if the rules are set in advance and both partners understand them. Why, do you disagree?'

'I don't know. I've never thought about it.' Kelly stared back at her friend. 'It sounds like a pretty mercenary way to behave.'

'I'm not talking about adultery or about hurting people. I'm talking about sex between two mature, consenting, free adults. I don't think there's anything wrong with that.'

'No, but...' Kelly swallowed, not really sure what she'd been about to say, because she realised that she didn't think there was anything wrong with what Sarah was saying, either. When she was younger and more romantic she'd have argued automatically that love had to be a prerequisite for sex — at least for her. But her marriage had taught her that love was not a wonderful thing. Being in love didn't protect you. It didn't stop you being hurt or betrayed, it merely made the pain worse when it happened.

She pushed her hair away from her shoulders, tilted her

head and stared at Sarah. 'So, what are you recommending? That I march up to Jack McEwan and propose a quickie in the common room?'

Sarah laughed. 'Well, I know I would,' she said expansively. 'If I was single I wouldn't be able to resist the temptation to do something along those lines. And Margie's already admitted that she'd be tempted if she wasn't married.'

'I said I'd be tempted,' Margie intervened lightly. 'I didn't say I'd do anything about it.'

'So you *do* think sex without commitment is immoral,' said Kelly.

'Not immoral,' Margie answered. 'Just not necessarily wise.' Her gaze turned introspective. 'I remember once, briefly, thinking I might be able to have an affair with Ben and walk away unscathed.'

Kelly asked, 'And what happened?'

'He didn't like it.' Margie sent her a flat look. 'He wouldn't have it. I don't mean to rain on your parade, Sarah, but I suspect Jack McEwan and Ben have quite a lot in common. You'd have to take care, Kelly.'

Kelly turned cold but Sarah's cheerful laugh broke the tension. 'Don't listen to her,' Sarah ordered. 'Ben was after Margie for months before she finally gave in, everyone knew that. He'd never have let you go, whatever you said, Margie. This is an entirely different situation. Jack barely knows Kelly. That's why she should move now. Before he gets to know her. Before friendship or familiarity get in the way.'

'I do find him attractive,' Kelly mused, Sarah's confidence reassuring her again. This *was* completely different. 'But we also have to work together. Wouldn't it get awkward?'

'Why?' Although Margie, she saw, looked unsure again, Sarah finished her muffin, pushed her plate away and took a mouthful of Diet Coke then answered for both of them. 'The man's been around. He'll know how to handle it. He's still working alongside the nurses on Maui ward without a problem, isn't he? I heard he's had half of them already.'

Kelly choked on her bread. 'That has to be an exaggeration,' she spluttered, once she had her breath back. 'At least I hope it is. He hasn't, has he? Not in four weeks. Though they do seem to like him on the ward.'

'Who knows how much is true and how much is rumour?' Sarah's shrug was philosophical. 'All I know for sure, is that four days after he started work here he had, and I mean *had*, Bobby's PA in the back seat of his Porsche,' she declared. 'And I can say that with absolute certainty, because three eye-witnesses saw him come out of there with his shirt in shreds. Plus, Veronica's embroidered his name on that black cape she wears, and she told Bobby once that she only ever does that when she's actually *you-know-what-ed* a man.'

'I'm not sure that you could actually have sex in a Porsche,' Kelly said cautiously. She'd heard the same story, as well as Jack McEwan's denials. But the car park had been full that morning, and she'd had to leave her car outside her colleague's townhouse and – just out of curiosity, of course – she'd peeked inside the car on her way past. 'It's very cramped in the back. The seat's tiny, there's barely room for a child.'

'And accusing anyone of *having* Veronica might be taking it a bit far, Sarah,' Margie scolded lightly. 'I can't imagine her being the passive sort. She wouldn't have needed to be talked into anything. No wonder his shirt ended up ripped, he wouldn't have had a chance of getting away once she decided to bury those amazing nails in him.'

'Whatever.' Sarah laughed. 'Maybe he likes his play rough, who can tell? It's almost two,' she added, gathering the remnants of their lunches on to her tray. 'I'll have to get to my clinic or all hell will break lose. Kelly, you will think about it, won't you? Where's the harm? If I was single, you wouldn't be able to keep me away from him!'

'I'll let it percolate.' Kelly smiled back. 'Though I have to say I don't understand why he seems tempting. Promiscuity's not supposed to be an appealing trait in a man any more, especially now we know how dangerous it can be. Yet here we are, talking about the man as if I should maybe sample him, the same way I might try a new shampoo. Frankly, it doesn't sound right, and it certainly isn't the way I was brought up to behave.'

Sarah put an arm around her as they walked out towards the hospital corridor. 'Think about it, my love. If you're going to take the plunge anyway, you may as well choose someone who'll make the effort worthwhile. With his history, the man has to be seriously skilled.'

'Pity the poor woman he eventually marries,' Kelly said with a shudder.

'He might reform,' Margie argued.

'They never do.' Kelly felt her face go tight. 'Marriage doesn't curb serial womanisers, the danger of discovery just adds extra spice to their affairs.'

She saw Sarah and Margie exchange looks, and bit her lip immediately, cross with herself as she realised that they'd be making assumptions based on her bitter remark. She never discussed her marriage, that wasn't her way, but she knew that Sarah, particularly, had always been curious. She wished she'd kept her mouth shut.

'Not that I'm talking about exchanging any vows here,' she added hastily. She hoped that one day she would find someone to spend the rest of her life with – the alternative still felt a little too lonely for her to accept just yet. But if she did remarry, then she wasn't going to be stupid enough to make the same mistakes again. She wouldn't be looking for a man like Jack McEwan. One womanising husband was enough for any woman per lifetime. She'd never voluntarily put herself through that sort of pain again. 'We were talking fun, weren't we?'

'Sure.' After a brief hesitation, Sarah grinned. 'Fun.'

Kelly smiled back, checked her watch and realised she only had a couple of minutes left before her first clinic patient was due to be seen. She said hasty farewells and rushed away. She skipped, taking the steps two at a time, then walked fast through the link area between the two wings of the hospital into the main foyer on the paediatric side and beyond into the toy-strewn Outpatient area.

Waving and calling out 'Hello' to the collection of small children and parents waiting in the central play area, she hurried through into the nearest office.

She drew up swiftly when she saw Jack sitting behind the desk she normally used herself for the session. He was leafing through the top stack of notes on the desk, but at her entrance he looked up, his eyes swiftly scanning with approval the figure standing in front of him.

It should have been annoying, she knew. Even given the conversation she'd just had about the man, it should still have been irritating that he seemed to see her primarily as a sexual being, and only secondly as a professional colleague. Only she wasn't irritated at all. Her eyes drifted automatically to his shoulders. She felt...warm.

He was dangerous, she knew that. It would be like playing with fire. But maybe the best way to neutralise the danger was to tame it. And maybe the best way to do that would be to harness it, bend it and use it in a way that suited her?

Because there was no getting away from the basic facts. Jack McEwan was a *very* sexually attractive man. The strong aura of sensuality surrounding him reminded her just how long…how *very* long it had been since she'd last felt the tender warmth, and the comfort of a man's arms about her. And, she acknowledged then, quite unable to tear her eyes away from his strong, masculine body, he made her want to experience that feeling once again.

chapter four

'Sorry.' Jack's lazy grin was so warm and welcoming that Kelly's heart missed a beat.

Taken aback, she wondered if he'd meant sorry for the way he'd looked at her, and she didn't know what to say about that. But his, 'I've done it again, haven't I?' made her realise he was apologising for taking her examination room again, quite accidentally, the same way he had when he'd arrived during the morning session.

He pushed back from the desk and stood up. 'This is your preferred room in the afternoons too, is it? I'll move.'

'No, don't. Please stay. It doesn't matter.' Her breathlessness, she knew, was as much a reaction to his presence, as it was to her haste in running back to the department. She waved him to sit. 'I'll take the next room. I don't mind. They're all the same anyway.' Her throat felt dry and she swallowed to clear it. 'I was hoping to speak to you actually. I wondered if you were busy after work. Because if you aren't, and if you would like to see something of the local area, then I'd be happy to give you a tour.'

To her it sounded like a simple, straightforward offer; the sort of offer anyone would make to a stranger coming to a new place to live. But his mesmerising tea-green eyes zeroed in so sharply on hers that she had the impression she'd startled him.

'A tour,' he echoed. 'You're offering me a tour?'

Only that morning she'd told him how little free time

she had, she remembered. He was probably surprised she could spare any. And she couldn't really. Not after being away for so long. She had a lot of catching up to do in the paperwork department, and she also had to ring round and confirm that she had locum work organised for her free weekends over the next month. But she could make a few hours tonight. It was only fair, she rationalised. It had nothing to do with anything Sarah had just said. The man was new to the area, and it was...well, it was only polite that she should try to be...hospitable.

'I know this part of Wellington pretty well,' she went on. 'I could point out the best shopping areas and the gardens. I could also show you Thorndon, there are some good cafés worth knowing about there. Or if you've already seen that part of town, we could even drive out to the beach at Makara, if you feel like a bit of evening exercise.'

It was years since she'd been there herself, but the thought of the peaceful beach and the rocky, isolated shoreline was suddenly overwhelmingly appealing. 'It's quiet there during the week,' she added. 'We'd have the place to ourselves.'

'What sort of exercise did you have in mind?'

'Walking.' The way his eyes narrowed down made her bite her lower lip. Surely...surely he didn't think she was propositioning him? 'You could swim if you wanted, but it'll be pretty cold, even at this time of year.'

Oh, God, she thought. He was probably so used to women coming on to him, he automatically assumed they always were. The thought that she possibly was...perhaps...building up to that, multiplied her discomfort. She hadn't meant to leap right in, but the thought had been there, she knew, in a roundabout sort of way, and she felt her colour deepen.

'If we get away early enough to give us plenty of daylight, there's a great walk out around the shoreline,' she continued, speaking fast now. 'Nothing adventurous, even I can manage it, but it's pretty. The best way back is up over farmland into the hills. There's a proper farm track so it's easy walking, but it climbs quite a lot, which is what makes it such good exercise.'

She stopped then, self-conscious, knowing that she was blabbering and what's more, that he knew it.

'I'd like that.'

'Oh. Oh, good.' After all the build up, she hadn't expected that. She'd been steeling herself for an excuse. Now she didn't know what to do. So she gave him a big, wide, confident smile. 'Great.'

'After clinic then?'

'Sure.' She took one step back in the direction of the door, then stopped. 'Jack?' He looked up from his notes. 'We could have a meal afterwards.' What did that mean? she asked herself, shocked at her behaviour. She couldn't possibly be...was she actually asking this man out? Tonight? Surely she wasn't *that* desperate. Or, was she? 'Only...er...only if you wanted to, of course,' she added lamely.

There was a brief, tight silence and then he said, 'That sounds fun.'

'Great.' The surge of excitement she felt, alarmed her. She was being ridiculous, Kelly told herself with mounting panic. She wasn't a schoolgirl. But maybe she was regressing, because the hand she reached out to the door was clearly shaking with nerves, and she found herself jerking the door open with clumsy haste.

At the end of clinic, the staff generally met in the main

office for afternoon tea. Kelly was called out to talk to a patient's father at the end of her list, and when she came back the junior doctors had left for a teaching session, while the nurses who'd helped with the session were packing up.

Two minutes later she was alone with Jack. She waited while he packed up the last of the notes he'd been studying. 'How's your ICU patient doing this afternoon?' she asked, doing her best to keep this interaction strictly normal, when she suddenly realised that what – alarmingly – she really felt like doing was hauling him into one of the consulting rooms and tearing off his clothes.

Oh, God – you've got to get a grip on yourself, Kelly. You're sick, she lectured herself grimly. Major, big time, seriously sick!

'Slight improvement.'

Her mouth quirked at the thought of how much less nonchalant he might have sounded if he knew what she was really thinking.

'If you don't mind, I'd like to check on her now before we go along to Maui Ward.'

'Of course I don't mind.' The clinical talk sobered Kelly. She'd visited Cindy, his child with septicaemia from the meningitis bacteria, several times during her night on call. 'I'd like to see her too.'

They discussed Cindy's case on their way to the Intensive Care Unit, before they each pulled on a surgical gown over their outside clothes. To get into Cindy's cubical in the isolation part of the unit they added another gown, as well as a mask and gloves.

The child's parents stood to greet them, and Kelly was relieved to see that they looked as if they'd at least had time to grab a change of clothes since she'd last visited them, in the early hours of the morning.

'The nurses showed us where we could have a nap and a shower,' Cindy's father explained when Jack asked them if they'd managed to have a break or time for a meal. 'And they've been bringing us food, we just haven't had any appetite.'

Still in a coma and requiring a breathing machine, Cindy was connected to a multitude of monitors and infusions. Kelly was used to looking after children in Intensive Care but even to her experienced eyes the child amongst all the machinery looked terrifyingly tiny and frail. The spotted purple rash that Kelly knew she'd started before coming into hospital had coalesced into blotchy stains across her legs and stomach. But Kelly thought the rash seemed less angry than it had the night before.

'The surgical doctors used a special machine on her legs, Dr McEwan. To measure her pulses.' Cindy's mother waited until the greetings were over and Jack had examined Cindy. 'They told us they wanted to consult with you before they made any decisions, but they said things were looking a little better than this morning.'

Kelly saw the older woman swallow heavily and from the way her husband's face creased and the arm he put around his wife's back trembled, she could tell how hard it was for them.

Jack crouched down beside the little girl's mother.. 'There are definite signs of improvement,' he reassured them. 'I realise things don't look very different on the surface and it's too early to make any guarantees,' his eyes met Kelly's and she knew he meant that it was still too early to be sure that Cindy would survive. 'But we're definitely more optimistic tonight than we were this time yesterday.'

'We feel so helpless.' Cindy's mother raised a hand to accept the box of tissues Jack passed to her, and dabbed at her eyes. 'On Sunday she was fine, apart from a few aches and pains and a bit of a temperature. When she started getting those purple spots on her legs I called the doctor straight away, but I never dreamed it could be anything to do with meningitis.'

'It's a terrifyingly unpredictable infection,' Jack acknowledged.

Kelly agreed. And in Cindy's case the classic signs of meningitis, like headache and stiffness in her neck, had been absent. Her strain of the illness was rare, and also very lethal, although Cindy had received a dose of antibiotic from her family doctor, and was on her way to the hospital in an ambulance within an hour of the first signs of a rash developing. In a less severe disease, that response would have been good enough.

They spent some time with the family, and she noticed that Jack took care to make sure that there were no outstanding concerns before they left. Then they went around the rest of their patients on the ward, handed over to the doctors on call for the night, before stopping on Maui Ward to check the day's X-rays.

'Did you always want to look after children?' she asked Jack curiously. He obviously enjoyed it, but aside from cases like Cindy's, children's medicine generally lacked the drama of other areas. She could picture him equally well working in Trauma perhaps. Or Neurosurgery or Emergency.

He changed films. 'My childhood dream was to become an astronaut,' he confessed with a grin. 'Before I started varsity, I thought seriously about joining the Air Force. But when I ended up studying medicine, I had no problem in quickly deciding to specialise in children's medicine. How about you?'

'I was initially keen on working in Obstetrics, but I switched after my first year.'

'Too many sleepless nights?'

'In the eighteen months until the end of that year, I suffered three miscarriages,' she said as matter-of-factly as she could. 'It started hurting seeing all those happy mothers. Switching to looking after children gave me the contact with kids, without the poignancy bit kicking in every time.'

She stopped then, and stiffened, utterly shocked at herself. 'I can't believe I just told you that,' she gasped. 'I can't *believe* I blurted that out, like that.'

'Can you still have children? If you want to?'

'I don't know.' She shook her head. 'It's not relevant anyway. I'm divorced.'

'You wouldn't marry again?'

Her mouth compressed. 'Not any time soon.'

'That bad?'

'It had its moments.' She looked down. 'I don't know for sure biologically about pregnancy, but I know it would be very hard to go through all those months of waiting again,' she went on jerkily. 'I lost the last baby during my second trimester, when I'd started to feel secure. They never found out why, but it was a painful experience emotionally. And if I never have children of my own, my job will compensate me a little for that. It's probably warped to say this, but I get complete joy out of taking care of children the way we do.'

She was still reeling that she'd given so much away. And to a man she barely knew! Other than her ex-husband, she'd never once discussed her miscarriages and her reason for changing direction in her career. Clearly Jack's gift for drawing out children worked on adults too.

'It's not warped.' He spoke slowly, considering the problem.. 'It's a very natural reaction. You're needed here and you do a good job. It's perfectly normal to feel fulfilled in those circumstances. You should enjoy it – not try to deny it. Be happy.'

'I am,' she declared stoutly. 'Of course, I am.' But the full truth forced its way out. 'Well, most of the time, anyway.'

'Have you talked to a specialist? Recently? Advances happen. Thinking changes.'

'I'm not in any position to think about babies,' she said firmly. How could she? Especially when her priority this year was work – and lots of it. Fearful of what else she might reveal, she grabbed for another file. 'Oh, this baby might interest you.' While her specialist area of expertise was childhood cancer, Jack's special interest was infectious diseases. 'Roger admitted her shortly before I went on leave with a very severe post-measles pneumonia...'

'Roger asked me to see her, and I took over her care three weeks ago,' he said smoothly, sliding the file away from her and dropping it back on to the pile she'd grabbed it from. 'She's fine. I saw her last week in clinic and she's thriving. Are we finished?'

'I suppose so.' She felt strangely awkward and uneasy. 'I was thinking. About the walk.' Suddenly it did not seem like a good idea to have too much time for talking. But she didn't want to cancel the evening, she discovered. Besides, that wouldn't be sensible, she told herself firmly. She didn't want him to guess how nervous she was, particularly about how much she'd told him about her past. Quite apart from anything else, it wouldn't be polite.

'By the time we get out to Makara and set off on the walk, there might not be enough time to finish before it's dark,' she explained. 'The last thing this place needs is for one of us to fall in a rabbit hole, requiring time off work with a broken ankle.' But then dinner would mean plenty of talking time as well. 'How…er…how would you feel about going to a movie?'

He studied her steadily for a few seconds and she had a sudden, quite disconcerting sensation that he saw right through every excuse. 'Which one?'

'Oh, there are quite a few on.' She had no idea what any of them were about, of course, since it was years since she'd last seen a film. But the cinemas were mostly multi-screen ones nowadays, and she was sure they'd find something suitable.

She insisted they took her car. After the highly erotic dream she'd had the night before, she didn't feel ready for the Porsche. He eyed the dented bumper doubtfully, and raised his brows when she apologised for the passenger door – making him climb over her seat to get into his. Unfortunately, as she explained, the lock had become jammed ever since someone had backed into her in a supermarket car park, but he made no comment.

She chose a large, multi-screen complex in the centre of town. Excluding children's films and unless they wanted to wait two hours for a true-life drama that Kelly would have been quite interested in seeing, the choice was between a comedy romance – a term of absolute irony, she thought acidly – and an action movie.

The romance had been showing for five minutes already, ruling it out as far as she was concerned. But even if the timing had been perfect, there would have been no contest. Automatically she ordered tickets for the action film but Jack double-crossed her by overruling her at the box office and handing across cash while she was still fumbling to find her debit card. Two minutes later, she found herself being ushered into the romance.

The screen was still showing promotions for upcoming movies so they hadn't missed anything, but he must have sensed her puzzlement because when he handed her an ice cream, he raised a quizzical eyebrow. 'Will it be so bad?'

'I'm just surprised. And if you went for it because you thought I secretly wanted it, you made a big mistake,' she said in a low voice. 'I'm not the romantic type. Be warned. If it gets slushy, I may vomit.'

He grinned. 'I want to see it.'

As she took a bite of her ice-cream and made a scoffing sound, his grin widened.

'Cynic,' he accused. 'Is it so inconceivable that I just might be a romantic?'

'Totally inconceivable,' she confirmed.

The movie wasn't as bad as she was expecting. The story involved a case of mistaken identity and a series of misunderstandings culminating in a predictable, happy-ever-after wedding. But the acting was skilled and the humour deft.

She was less keen on the sex scenes. The lovemaking was passionate and explicit and the actor was tall, dark and very attractive, and he reminded her uncomfortably of Jack. Any other time, she recognised, she might have enjoyed that synergy, but not with the man himself sitting beside her. She felt self-conscious. She was aware from time to time of him watching her, and she took care during the sex scenes to stare straight ahead and not fidget too obviously.

After the movie, when they'd filed out with the crowd

down concrete stairs and out on to the street, she met his amused look irritably. 'Of course in real life she'd have married the brother. He was far nicer. He would have made a much better husband.'

'She wasn't in love with the brother.'

'Love.' Kelly rolled her eyes. 'Spare me. Maybe you weren't kidding? Maybe you really are a romantic?'

'Of course, I am.' He laughed at her expression. 'All men are romantics. How else would the species survive? Let's eat.'

They had cheese and pineapple burgers in a café near the cinema. There was live jazz and it was crowded and noisy and Kelly was glad because, beyond shouted questions and comments on the music and the meal, it was impossible to hold any sort of conversation. The food was astonishingly good. Her burger was perfect and the chips were thick and crisp on the outside and fluffy inside, exactly the way she liked them.

Neither of them wanted dessert. Jack had a beer and then another and she ordered Cokes and they sat back after their meals and enjoyed the music. When the band finished she checked her watch and saw, to her astonishment, that it was almost one. She could hardly believe it. The evening had flown by. In fact, she suddenly realised that it was years since she'd been out this late.

She paid the bill by the simple expedient of having her card out and ready, and getting to the counter before Jack. She noticed that he wasn't happy about the situation, but to her relief he didn't argue the point and merely thanked her for the meal.

Kelly knew that she'd have to work an extra shift to cover the cost. However, she didn't often go out and it somehow felt important that she was able to pay her way.

It was a ten-minute walk from the café to her car, but he seemed not to mind and she was grateful for that. The medical centre where she sometimes worked had issued her a pass for the parking area, meaning that was one expense she was able to avoid.

On the drive back to Karori she remembered, belatedly, the original intentions of the outing and she made an effort to point out the different suburbs and landmarks like the Gardens and the Karori shopping centre. She parked in Hospital Road outside his home and got out of the car so he could climb over her seat.

As soon as they'd come to a halt, she'd suddenly felt extraordinarily nervous. And now, standing beside the car, she found herself gazing hesitantly up at him, not sure whether or not it was normal to offer a goodnight kiss after such an evening. She wouldn't have minded a quick one, or maybe even a slow one, she thought, feeling her legs go a little shaky at the prospect. Or even – and she was shocked at the strength of her need and desire – a very, *very* slow kiss. But Jack simply pecked her cheek and tangled his fingers loosely in a few strands of her hair.

'Thanks. That was fun.' He lifted his hand and let the blonde strands fall free of his fingers. 'See you in the morning?'

'On the wards. Yes.'

'You have beautiful hair.'

'It's too long.' She felt herself colour. 'I keep meaning to get it cut but I never get around to it. Bye then.' Disappointed when he did nothing more, with her cheek still buzzing a little where he'd briefly pressed his lips, she got back into the car.

But Jack knocked on her window. 'Kelly?' She wound

her window right down. 'Don't. Don't cut it. Leave it just as it is.'

His eyes were dark, very intense, and she felt her pulse jerk. She swallowed heavily. 'OK.'

'Are you still in love with your ex-husband?'

'Warwick?' She shook her head, confused. 'I haven't seen him for years. He lives in Europe now.'

'Was that a no?'

'Yes.' It came out in a burst, and she felt herself flushing again. 'No. I mean, yes...yes, it was a no.' She felt ridiculous suddenly. Awkward, like a child. 'Warwick is out of my life now for good.'

'Why don't we do that beach trip tomorrow, after work?'

'There's a meeting all afternoon in town. It may run late.' Which would make it too late for the beach by the time she got back out to Karori.

'I remember now. I'm going too.' He smiled but his expression was mostly watchful. 'Thursday then?'

Kelly wondered if she was really ready for this. 'I'll let you know,' she promised. 'In the morning.'

Only the next morning she didn't feel any less nervous. When she'd been junior and inexperienced, sometimes on her way to work, she'd felt apprehension and worry like this – as if there were a thick worm slowly turning in the bottom of her stomach. From time to time, when a child was dying and she had to face the family, knowing that there was nothing more she could do to help alleviate their suffering, the feeling came back again. But now it was her new colleague, not her job, which was worrying her.

She still wasn't sure what she was going to say to him. He's just a man, she reminded herself for the umpteenth time, turning on her headlights as she drove underneath the barrier into the hospital's underground car park. She wasn't a child any more. She would cope. Sarah was right to suggest that it was time she acknowledged the sexual side of her nature again. But saying that firmly to herself was one thing – actually doing something about it, was quite another. She had, after all, been brought up quite strictly. And, if there was one thing that 'nice girls' didn't do – it was to proposition strange men! Not that Jack was exactly a stranger, of course. He was, after all, a colleague whose work she admired.

Besides, she'd already gone too far down the track to back out now, she told herself nervously. Her unconscious knew it – she couldn't remember precise details of the dream which she'd had two nights in a row, but she knew it was sexual and she knew Jack and his Porsche had featured on both nights – even if her conscious brain was less enthusiastic. Knowing her luck, if she chickened out now she'd probably end up by becoming totally obsessed with him. So, maybe her best option was to try and get the itch out of her system.

And being able to handle an affair, even one as short and sharp as the one she was contemplating, would at least prove that she was now able to draw a line under her unhappy marriage, and move on.

It all made perfect sense.

So, why did she still feel a mass of nerves and deep apprehension?

She was scheduled to meet Jack and their junior doctors for an examination of all the team's patients on Maui Ward at eight-thirty. It was now only just eight o'clock, and she knew that her registrar wouldn't be in for another half-hour. But Jack, looking sexy and relaxed in cream slacks,

Jack of Hearts 57

tan belt and a casual open-necked, soft yellow shirt, was already there. He was standing half-way down the ward with Tania, the ward's nurse manager.

Tania was an enthusiastic and forward-thinking woman. Not only was she ideal for her job, but on both personal and professional levels Kelly liked her very much. In fact, there was no reason in the world why Tania shouldn't be flirting with the tall, handsome consultant, but it still came as a jolt.

Kelly found herself coming to an abrupt halt just inside the main doors. The two were enjoying themselves too much to notice her, and she watched them for a few moments. She noted the way Tania let her hand rest familiarly on Jack's arm and then his chest, as she laughed up at some teasing remark he'd made. And she saw that Tania's eyes were sparkling in a way Kelly hadn't seen them do for a long time.

Tania glanced her way and then did a double take, before calling out with flushed cheeks, 'Hi, Kelly!' and looking slightly self-conscious as she quickly removed her hand from where it rested against the paediatrician's chest.

Just *what* did Tania think she was doing, draping her arms around Jack? Kelly wondered as she walked towards them. She'd heard talk about Tania and Jack on her first day back at work. But, knowing how upset Tania had been since the recent break-up of her marriage, Kelly had dismissed the speculation as silly gossip.

'Hi there!' Tania went on brightly. Far *too* brightly, Kelly told herself grimly. 'I didn't hear you come in. Jack's been telling me silly stories about his hospital in London. One of the children brought his pet rat on to the ward. He kept it hidden in a box in his cupboard, only one night it escaped and jumped on to the night nurse's lap and she almost had a heart attack. The staff didn't realise it was a pet and the whole unit had to be evacuated for fumigation. Can you imagine the horror job of moving all those kids?'

'Doesn't sound much fun,' Kelly commented. She put a smile on her face and nodded a greeting to her colleague who, after an initial friendly nod, now studied her enigmatically enough to suggest he'd sensed her disquiet. But she was happy for Tania, she told herself firmly. And they should all be grateful to Jack for making the manager laugh again. She just hoped Tania knew better than to take him seriously. And, quite why she should suddenly be feeling low and depressed, she had absolutely no idea.

'Don't mind me, I'm early,' she said easily, when the consultant moved as if to follow after her towards the nursing station. 'I didn't mean to interrupt. In fact I didn't even mean to come on to the ward. I don't know why I'm here.' She turned about. 'I might grab a coffee before we start. Jack, I'll meet you back here with the others in half…'

'I'll come,' he interjected. 'Tania, what about you?'

'Too much work to be done,' the manager told him. 'I've a stack of stuff in my in-tray and I've already held you up far too long as it is. See you two soon.'

Considering what she'd just witnessed, the strength of her physical awareness of Jack behind her as they took the central stairs up to the medical staff room bothered Kelly quite a lot. 'I like your after-shave,' she commented, focusing on specifics. In two days she'd come to associate the woody scent with him. 'What's the fragrance? Pine?'

'The bottle's blue, that's all I know.' He leaned around her to open the door for her, his arm brushing her shoulder in the process, and sending disruptive tendrils of heat streaking along her collar bone to her throat. 'My mother gave it to me for Christmas. The advertising promises it sends women wild.'

'Oh, I'm sure it does!' Kelly murmured caustically, feeling her lips tightening. 'But then I'm equally sure you don't need after-shave to do that.' She jerked her gaze away when his turned to look at her, his gaze curious and speculative. 'I can't imagine you with a mother. What's she like?'

'Kind, loving, motherly and sweet, with a core of steel. My parents run a property outside Palmerston,' he added, and she guessed that he meant Palmerston North, a town to the north of Wellington, rather than the small town with a similar name in southern New Zealand.

Kelly spooned coffee into mugs and added water from the kettle. 'Not an easy life.' She didn't know, really – she was a city girl through and through, she'd never even been on a farm – but that seemed to be the conventional thing people said about the business.

'They love it.'

'That's good to hear. It was also good to hear Tania laughing again.' She carried his drink across and met his quizzical look frankly this time. 'The way you looked at me downstairs, I thought you might be thinking I disapproved. I wanted to say, for the record, that I don't. I think it's fine.'

His dark head tilted slightly. 'But?'

So she'd been right about him being intuitive. There was a 'but', of course, although why she should feel it was important to point it out, was beyond her at the moment.

'Tania's been badly hurt recently. I'd never dream of discussing that normally,' Kelly told him. 'But you might not have been here long enough to understand what's been going on in her life. I know she's still feeling delicate emotionally, because any woman would. I hope that, whatever's going on between the two of you, you'll bear that in mind.'

'If you mean her husband leaving her for another woman, then I know,' he said slowly. 'Tania told me about that. You don't think I'd be sensitive to her feelings?'

'Oh, I'm quite sure you would be.' She concentrated on her drink. She suspected he'd be very sensitive. But that might not help. She remembered the way she'd confided in him herself. 'Women tell you lots of things, don't they?'

'Dr West,' he chided, 'you've been listening to gossip again.'

Her head came up sharply and she flushed at his knowing look. 'I see what I see.'

'What is it with this place?' He shook his head. 'Don't people have lives of their own to worry about? I have a quiet, friendly chat with a woman and suddenly...'

'You're a good-looking, unattached, heterosexual man. You're very sure of yourself, and you were stupid enough to get caught having sex with Veronica Hay in your car, in broad daylight,' she reminded him, bemused that he still refused to accept the implications of that. 'Of course, there's going to be gossip!'

'I told you, it wasn't like that...'

'That's not my point,' she interjected. 'It's nothing to do with me *what* you and Veronica, or you and Tania, or you and whoever-else-you-take-a-fancy-to-this-week do to each other. I'm simply reminding you that there are reasons why people are going to talk. A piece of friendly advice: if you don't like the gossip, start thinking with your head and not your...'

'Libido?'

'If you like.' Kelly met his exasperated look square on. 'If you used your head, you'd realise that you have to be discreet around here. This isn't some huge American or English institution, it's a small New Zealand hospital. People notice things here. You have to learn to be careful. For instance if, *and only if*, I've misunderstood your involvement with Tania and it isn't the way it looks – and *if* you were by chance interested in me, it would be important to me that no one here found out anything about us. I would insist on absolute discretion, and...'

'Whoa – stop! Pull back a second.' He put up his hand, clearly startled. 'Did you just proposition me...?'

Her fingers closed convulsively around her cup, utterly shocked at her own behaviour. Oh, Lord! There was not doubt that she *had* just openly propositioned him. Goodness knows what she thought she'd been doing, but that was *precisely* what she'd done! It seemed that while she'd been dithering about what she was going to do, her subconscious had gone ahead and made all the arrangements. So, what in the hell was she supposed to say or do now?

'If...if I did...er...proposition you,' she ventured nervously, 'would you be interested?'

Under the deliberate, cool appraisal with which he was now regarding her, Kelly realised that she'd just made an utter fool of herself. Frantically praying that the earth would somehow open up, allowing her to quickly disappear from sight, she was astonished by his immediate response.

'Of course, I would.' His gaze swept quickly over her hair, her breasts and then her legs, before finally returning to her face again. 'But you know that. You must be used to men being interested. What's the hurry?'

She drew in a quick, courage-gathering breath. 'Why waste time?' she said, deliberately offhand. 'You're interested. I'm interested. We're adults, aren't we?'

'It must have been almost love at first sight for you?'

He was teasing her, she realised. She smiled. 'A different L word.'

'Shame.' He almost looked sincere. If she was meeting him for the first time, with no background knowledge, she knew she might have been worried by that. 'The first one would have made life easier.'

'Not mine.' It would have made her life unbearable. Her smile was firmly in place now. 'And since whatever happens we'll still have to work together, I think strict honesty is appropriate.'

'Honesty?' He sounded thoughtful. 'There's a novel concept. Are you sure about that?'

'Totally sure.' She tilted up her chin. 'So Tania...?'

'Is still very much in love with her husband.'

'Veronica...?'

'Nothing happened.'

'No one else?'

'Not at present.'

'Well, then.' She hesitated for a moment.

She *could* do this, she told herself firmly. Of course, she could. She wasn't a young girl any longer, but a reasonably sophisticated woman. A woman who'd been married, divorced, and who was definitely *not* looking for commitment. So, everything would be light and amusing and teasing and casual; exactly the way it was now, and she'd be fine.

'Why...er...don't we start by going into town together, this afternoon?' she said as lightly as she could. The meeting they were scheduled to attend was a regular three-monthly teaching and administrative session for doctors. 'We can take your car. I've been wondering for a couple of days,' she added, amazed to hear herself sounding so incredibly, so miraculously calm. 'I've been wondering if there really *is* room to make love in a Porsche?'

chapter five

Jack had been propositioned before in his life. Plenty of times. But never like that. Never so boldly, so directly and unambiguously, yet at the same time with such delicate tenseness underneath. The dichotomy between Kelly's superficial sexual confidence and her underlying disquiet intrigued him.

She was doing her best to conceal her nervousness behind laughter, and the cheery air of dismissive unconcern she cultivated so well. But he wasn't easily taken in. Despite the poised self-assurance of her approach, anxiety still lingered in the secret, wary blue shadow at the back of her eyes every time she glanced at him. It was there when they met at morning clinic, and it was still there when she looked up sharply from the baby she was examining when he came to fetch her from the ward, reminding her that it was time to leave for town.

She talked brightly on their way out of the hospital grounds to where he'd parked his car, but the tension was still there. It underlay everything she said and did. When they came up to the car she sent him a very blue, challenging look and he raised his brows.

'I don't see the attraction with cars,' she declared. 'Aside from the macho, power thing, which obviously must appeal to you, I don't see why men make so much of them.' She flicked her fingers at the Porsche. 'This is pretty to look at, of course. But as far as I can see, the only difference between it and my little hatch-back, is that I don't have to think about all the hundred dollar notes in petrol and depreciation which I'm pouring down the drain every time I start mine up.'

The reminder of the battered little rust bucket which she called a car made him wince.

'If you don't see the difference, you need to drive it.' He put his key in the driver's door lock and activated the smooth, automatic retraction of the car's roof. It was a warm day, the sun was shining and unusually for Wellington, as he'd discovered, the breeze was only light. Just about perfect conditions for a topless ride.

He opened the driver's door for her. 'Get in. I'll adjust the seat.'

'I don't know what to do with automatics.'

'It's manual. Six gears instead of five.'

'Mine has four,' she said slowly. 'And it's very old. I've never driven anything with five gears, let alone anything new. Jack, I'm not sure...'

'Scared?'

'No.' Her chin hardened, but then it dropped. 'Maybe just a little,' she admitted. 'You know this is just wasted on me. I'm not a car fanatic.'

But she climbed in, looked around and her expression grew marginally more enthusiastic. 'Mmm, it's luxurious. I love the leather. The smell goes well with your pine. How fast does it go?'

'The speed limit.' He moved her seat forward. 'A hundred if you want to detour through town to try it out on the motorway.' The main road from Karori was only one lane each way and it was windy and invariably busy and there'd be no chance to stretch the car. 'If you do it right, it'll get you from standing to motorway speed in around five-and-a-half seconds. Put your belt on.'

'A hundred kilometres an hour in five-and-a-half seconds,' she echoed. 'Five-and-a-half *seconds*...? My car is more likely to take about five-and-a-half *weeks*!'

He smiled. 'You'll get the hang of it.'

'What about my hair?' She clicked in her belt then lifted her hands to her ponytail. She started tucking handfuls of hair inside the light jersey she wore. 'If it flies off in the wind, it'll go crazy.'

'There won't be any wind.' The Porsche's deflectors and side windows kept turbulence and noise almost as low when the top was down as when it was up. He walked around and climbed in beside her, lifted her hair out from under her collar, removed the fabric band and let the silken strands drop loose over her breasts. 'It's too gorgeous to be tied back, you should leave it loose all the time.

'Straight ahead then left at the corner,' he prompted, when she continued to stare at him with wide blue eyes. 'Right on to the road, then follow it all the way to the city.'

She blinked a few times then turned her head back to the front and braced her hands on the wheel. 'I know the way, thank you very much. I drive it every day.' She didn't say a thing about his gesture with her hair, but instead crinkled her brow and tried out the gears. 'This feels strange.'

'Relax.' Jack smiled. He put his sunglasses on, tipped his head back to the sun and closed his eyes. 'Just enjoy it.'

He didn't need to watch every second to know the moment when she began to do that. Till just before they reached the harbour, her handling felt nervous and she sat stiffly upright, clutching the wheel as if it was a life-buoy. But once she found her feet and realised the car would cling to the road whatever she did, Kelly settled down. She took the detour he suggested, turned on to the motorway and back towards the city, the drive from there on being smooth and fluid and close to expert.

She turned to look at him, and laughed when they slowed for the traffic queue through the tunnel where they came off the motorway. Two grinning men in a truck beside them tooted and blew kisses at her. 'This is incredible,' she proclaimed, waving back. 'This might just be the most fun I've ever had.'

'And we still have our clothes on!' He pushed his glasses higher and smiled at the suddenly nervous look the comment earned him. More proof, he realised, that she was not nearly as confident as she seemed determined to pretend. But flushed the way she was, her blue eyes wide and sparkling, and her glorious hair flowing free and wild, she looked young and alive and utterly enticing.

He meant to hold back. Despite the boldness of her approach he was determined to take it slowly with Kelly; anxious not to make any mistakes until he had figured her out. But a man would have to be a saint not to react to her like this. And since he'd never been a saint, he looked away.

'Pay attention,' he warned, nodding ahead. 'Your light's green.'

He'd only visited Wellington's main hospital in Newtown a couple of times since his appointment to Karori, and he was hazy on the sprawling geography of the place. But Kelly clearly knew her way around. He activated the switch on the centre console to close the roof as she parked, and then she showed him a short cut through the main hospital and into the academic area where the sessions were held.

They weren't the last to arrive but they weren't far from it, and he saw his arrival with Kelly attract interested looks from the staff already gathered. He didn't care what people thought or how they reacted, but she clearly did, because the instant she noticed the attention being paid to them, she swiftly left him, taking a seat on the other side of the lecture theatre.

The two hours were scheduled as an audit of general medical practice in the region, a time to focus on complications related to treatment in all paediatric and adult inpatients across the district for the six months up to the end of the previous year.

Jack had worked in Auckland until the week before Christmas so he didn't know the children they discussed and his role was largely advisory.

When it came to Kelly's turn, she detailed several cases, all children who'd died of cancer. Jack already admired Kelly for the dedication she brought to what was an incredibly emotionally demanding area of children's medicine. But as he listened to her skilled, precise recounting of every small detail of every case, he felt a surge of almost protective warmth. Her presentation was entirely professional but her controlled, careful delivery, so different from her normal lively, cheerful manner, told him that the memories of the children she'd lost still upset her. Kelly poured her very heart into her work, he realised.

He already knew that her patients and the rest of the staff at Karori adored her.

It wouldn't be hard to adore her himself.

When the meeting looked like running on far longer than it was scheduled to, Jack withdrew to the foyer and used his mobile to call Roger. The older doctor assured him there was no need to come back to Karori. 'It's been quiet all afternoon, we can hold the fort here. Kelly warned me you both might be late back, but tell her not to worry. She works too many hours as it is, plus I owe her around six weeks of nights for the times she's covered for me. You'll probably have to tie her down though to make her listen,' Roger added, sounding amused. 'Hey, but that could be fun.'

Jack rolled his eyes. 'Mind out of the gutter, Roger,' he said lazily. 'We're all working hard here.'

Kelly must have guessed what he was doing because when he returned to the main room she looked at him enquiringly and tapped her watch. He nodded to indicate there was nothing to worry about.

The meeting wound up finally around six but people lingered over coffee and sandwiches. Jack was glad of the opportunity to meet some of the Wellington staff for the first time. They discussed golf and the New Zealand cricket team's performance against the touring English side. Talking sport was fine with him, since the object was to get to know each other, not consult professionally, but Kelly's exasperated look as she happened in on the conversation made him smile.

One of the younger doctors, a confident-looking, dark-haired girl with a wide smile, came up to him as he was helping himself to fresh coffee. 'Dr McEwan, Jack, you probably don't remember me but we met three years ago in London when I was doing a paediatrics locum at Great Ormond Street. I introduced myself and we had a drink together. I'm from Palmerston North too.'

'I do remember.' Jack studied her face. 'Donna, isn't it? You were seeing some mad physiotherapist from Scotland.' He grimaced. 'A great huge chap with red hair who didn't like his girlfriend drinking with other men.'

'Your memory's good.' She laughed, and stroked her long hair. 'Angus. Yes, I'm sorry about that, he misunderstood. We broke up after that and I tried to call you a couple of times but I couldn't get through and then I changed hospitals. I thought about calling you up when I first heard you were coming to Karori, but I decided you'd have forgotten all about me.'

He had, until now. 'How long have you been back?'

'Too long. Are you enjoying New Zealand?'

'Very much.'

'You might find that fades,' she warned. 'I did. It's been great to be near family again, yes, but this country feels too small for me now. I'm planning to go away again as soon as I've finished my exams. Could we get together? I'd appreciate hearing your thoughts on where I should apply to in Britain.'

'Sure.' He was happy to give her his opinion on the various training programmes at hospitals he'd been associated with and he could give her the names of other doctors who might be able to help her with information on jobs. 'Give me a call at Karori.'

'What about tonight?'

'No.' Jack's eyes tracked automatically to the other side of the room where Kelly was involved in a discussion with two of Wellington's senior physicians. He tilted his head when, as if sensing his regard, she lifted her head and looked straight back at him unsmilingly. 'Not tonight.'

'Tomorrow then? Or I'm free Saturday night?'

He broke eye contact with Kelly and looked back at the registrar. 'Call me at work next week.'

'I'll give you my number.' She took a black pen out of her pocket and wrote a telephone number across the back of his hand. 'I will ring you at work but use this if you change your mind about the weekend.' Dark eyes sparkled up at him. 'I'm sorry about what happened with Angus that night,' she added. 'He ruined a perfectly enjoyable evening. I'd like the chance to make it up to you.'

Before he could respond they were interrupted by two other registrars wanting to talk to him about a child who was due to be admitted the next day into Karori under his care. By the time he'd worked through the details, Donna had moved on. Jack went across to where Kelly stood alone at the window. 'Ready?'

'I've been thinking about your car,' she mused. She didn't turn around. 'There's plenty of room to have sex in it. Not in the back, but the front's fine. You'd need to be creative, perhaps, but it wouldn't be difficult.'

'Why would you want to?' He watched her. 'It's cramped and indiscreet.'

'It would be discreet if you drove somewhere isolated.'

'Just admit the rumour's wrong,' he commanded. 'Admit nothing could have happened with Veronica in the hospital car park.'

'Do you care what people think?'

'Not especially. But that doesn't stop me wanting to salvage a fraction of my reputation with you. And if it's the car that turns you on, forget it. I'm not interested in making love to you furtively where we might be interrupted.'

'It's not the car.' Kelly knew she was flushing. 'I was curious, that's all.' She couldn't help herself glancing down sideways at the telephone number she'd watched Donna Ling write across his hand. 'Perhaps with Veronica you were so carried away with passion you forgot where you were?'

He caught at her hand and tugged her away from the glass. 'I'm not sixteen. Come on, we're almost the last ones left. Let's get out of here.'

Kelly let him keep hold of her hand because there was no one now to see them and the contact excited her. 'I thought we might go to my place.' She darted him a quick, experimental look. 'I warned Roger not to expect me back early, although I thought we'd have more free time than this. Did you talk to him personally before or the ward?'

'To him and he said not to bother coming back out. He'll make sure everything's OK at our end.'

Kelly felt guilty about taking up the other doctor's offer and she vowed to make it up to him. 'We can take longer then.'

'He'll call my mobile if he needs either of us in the meantime.'

'Fine.' They were almost at the car now, and she stopped and stared up at him. A curl of sensation unravelled slowly within her chest. 'I'll give you directions to Wadestown.'

'Hey,' he chided. 'Slow down.' He stroked her hair with his free hand. 'Don't we get to eat first?'

'I didn't think you'd have that much time.' She knew that sounded a tad waspish but once the words were out it was too late to re-think them. 'Because of Donna Ling.' She lifted the hand he still held and looked again at the number neatly written across the back of his. 'I assumed you'd be meeting her later. Or is she scheduled for tomorrow night?'

'I don't know.' He released her hand. 'I haven't thought about it. Want to drive again?'

'Your turn.' Kelly met his knowing look self-consciously. She'd enjoyed driving the car but it needed total concentration and she was jumpy now. 'I will have dinner with you but if you want somewhere flash then you'll have to take me home first because I might not get in wearing jeans.'

'I like you in jeans.' He unlocked the car. 'And you'll have to choose where we go because I don't know the place well enough yet.'

'Apart from last night it's probably two years at least since I've been to a restaurant.' Kelly tried to think. 'I know where there are supposed to be some good ones,' she said finally. She guided him to Queens Wharf, a development of restaurants and shops on the harbour downtown. It was a warm night, with hardly any wind, and from the converted timber warehouse where they chose to eat they could look out over the harbour and at the changing colours of the sky reflected in the sea as the sun started to set behind the city.

She had a glass of Riesling, just one, since although a couple more might have boosted the confidence, she still had to drive her car home from Karori. Jack had a beer. The grilled snapper they ordered was sweet and moist and they mopped up the juices with thick bread, and talked about work and he teased her about her driving and told stories about his travels and made her laugh.

He took her hand again in a casual way on the way back to the car. 'I don't want to rush away.'

Kelly directed him around the quays and through Oriental Bay, an expensive, harbour-side residential and restaurant area, and then up steep, winding streets and hairpin bends to the top of Mount Victoria. From there the light-speckled fingers of the city spread out beneath them between the dark, bush-strewn hills.

Although the air had been calm and warm down below, on the hill it was cooler and they had to fight the wind when they left the car. They climbed to the main viewing area at the top. 'If you follow this road down it winds almost straight back to the main hospital,' she shouted, showing Jack where she meant. 'And that's the university over that way beyond the city of course, Karori's up behind that. We can't see the hospital from here because of the hills, and that's where I live.' She pointed out the lights going up the hill off behind and to the right of the main business district.

She caught at her hair when the wind blew it high in the air, and she shivered a little in her thin, cotton jersey as she leaned forward to show him where they'd had dinner. Jack must have seen her shiver because he made a concerned sound and put a warm arm around her and hugged her close, away from the wind. The gesture was companionable, rather than sexual, but still the nerves across her back and arms and along her side tightened. 'This place isn't usually so deserted,' she told him, not needing to shout now. 'Usually there are tourists and young lovers all over the place.'

'Is this where you bring your lovers?'

'No.' She watched the view, not him.

'What about your husband?'

'We lived in Auckland. I came south just after my divorce.'

'How did you meet?'

'Classic story.' She hugged her head briefly against his arm to escape a fierce gust, and was surprised at her own daring. 'It was a friend's wedding. I was the bridesmaid and Warwick was best man. I fell in love with him over the wedding breakfast. At the time it seemed romantic.'

'And it doesn't now?'

She took a deep breath. 'Let's not talk about that.'

'Your call.' He turned her and cupped her face in his hands. 'Kelly?'

'Hmm?'

He lowered his head. 'Just this.'

It was a long time since Kelly had been kissed and although she'd been fantasising about him doing it, she still stiffened. But he was coaxing and persistent and warm and encouraging and he murmured for her to relax, and he praised her and whispered lovely words to her. He stroked her hair and gently worked her lips apart and as soon as she tasted him she started to remember how it could be. Her anxiety faded and she lost track of everything but the feeling of his mouth on hers and she started kissing him back.

Dimly she felt his hands shift from her hair to her shoulders, but he didn't try to undress her or touch her with any more intimacy than that. He let her put her arms around his neck and he supported her when her legs turned too weak to hold herself up, but he didn't bring her against him. Instead he seemed content just kissing her, her mouth, the corners of it, her top lip and her bottom, everywhere around her mouth, continually, ravishing her, alternately teasing and then languid, driving her out of her mind and leaving her hot and breathless and trembling.

Oblivious to the wind now or to headlights below them or the sounds of cars, she didn't hear anything, but Jack must have been more aware because he lifted his head away from her seconds before two couples came running up the steps to where they were.

Jack didn't speak, but he looked down at her heavily, then he slid his arm around her back again and steered her towards the steps, leaving the lookout for the newcomers.

Kelly felt dizzy. She stumbled, once or twice, on the

way down to the car, but he merely murmured something inaudible and supported her and stopped her falling.

He put her against the side of the Porsche while he found his key and unlocked the doors, then he took her cheeks in his hands again and kissed her lightly. 'All right?'

'Sort of,' she said numbly, when he lifted his head. But she felt slightly hysterical. 'Time to make love now?'

chapter six

Jack put his mouth to her ear. 'Stop rushing.'

'It's not rushing.' She was still having trouble breathing. 'I've known you three days.'

'More like two.' He moved back a little. His eyes were dark in his shadowed face. 'I like you, Kelly. I like what's happening here. But I don't want to push too fast.'

'It's not pushing.' She closed the gap between them, put her arms daringly around his waist. 'Don't get heavy on me, Jack. We're both aroused. We want to have sex. Let's keep it simple, hmm?'

But he drew back a little further, leaving her feeling bereft. 'Is that a less-than-roundabout way of telling me you want me for my body?'

He was amused, she realised gratefully. 'If that's how you want to put it,' she conceded. It was important there were no misunderstandings. 'It's not that I don't like you of course, but I don't have time in my life for anything serious now and even if I did you'd be…' She meant to say of course that he'd be one of the last men she'd consider, but the sharp way his eyes narrowed down made her think that that might not be wise. Instead she broke off. 'I really do not have the time right now for anything heavy' she concluded. 'I like you. Since we have to work together, it'd be good if we could be friends. So how about we go to bed together tonight, have a great time and then, well, be sort of casual about it tomorrow.'

'Casual.' He tapped her cheek lightly and she was

relieved to see that his expression was mocking rather than offended. 'You know, Kelly, you get more surprising every minute.'

'Well, this morning we agreed to be honest. It's a huge relief not to have to play silly games when we both know that all either of us wants is sex. I want to see you naked, Jack. Take me home and let's go to bed.'

'I'll take you home because I'm interested in seeing where you live. We'll talk about the rest.' He closed his eyes briefly then leaned forward again and put his mouth against her forehead. 'I haven't come prepared.'

'It's OK, I've got everything,' she said, quickly because she was embarrassed. Since she'd spent most of her marriage trying to get pregnant, this was the first time she'd had to consider contraception. 'I can offer you a choice of several boxes actually. Different colours.'

'Different colours.' She felt him smile then. 'Mmm.' His mouth moved and he kissed her left cheek. 'That sounds promising.'

Did it? She didn't know. She made some sound, a small sound with no meaning, but he seemed to find one there because he smiled again and stepped back and waited while she slid into the car.

It wasn't a long drive down from the hill and around the harbour and up into her suburb, but they seemed to get every red light going and it began to feel endless.

She cast Jack a quick, assessing look when they stopped for what felt like the umpteenth time going through town to wait for lights, then felt her face heat when he returned her look warmly.

He took his hand off the steering wheel and squeezed hers where it gripped her seat. 'OK?'

'Of course.' She stared at him. 'Why wouldn't I be?'

'If I had to put words to it, I'd say you seem determined yet apprehensive.' His eyes were shadowed inside the car but it wasn't so dark that she missed the perceptive appraisal in them. 'Am I right?'

She didn't like it that he could read her so easily. 'Don't worry about me. I know what I'm doing.'

He studied her silently for a few seconds, and she held her breath, but then he nodded slowly and returned his attention to the road ahead. When the lights changed to green he accelerated firmly away.

Her flat was a sixty-year-old, single-storeyed, two-bedroom wooden cottage on the high side of a narrow, winding street. The small garden – she loved gardening and happily she lived among neighbours who were happy to share cuttings and seeds so she was able to keep costs to a minimum – was bordered by a waist-high, white picket fence. She opened the gate for them and directed Jack in.

The light from the hall gleamed through the front door's lead-light glass and she saw his questioning look and explained, 'My flatmate's out tonight but she always leaves the lights on for security.' Absently she picked the heads off a couple of dahlias on her way up the path. 'We were burgled six months ago. I didn't have anything to lose, fortunately, but they took Geraldine's sound system and a couple of cameras.'

Jack frowned. 'You need an alarm.'

'Too expensive and the landlord said he wouldn't contribute. It's much cheaper to leave on a light.' She unlocked the door. She hoped he wouldn't judge her home's slightly shabby interior too harshly. The carpets were old, the walls needed painting and most of the furniture she owned was second- if not third-hand, but it was well loved and everything was clean and tidy, and what could gleam did.

Geraldine had left an electricity bill on the table just inside the door for her and Kelly saw the red print and flushed. She turned over the note hurriedly before Jack could see it. She had seven days, she knew, from today, to pay it. They never did cut you off of course, not that quickly, not as long as you contacted them, but the notice still embarrassed her and she wished she'd been the one to get to the mail first. She was used to it, this juggling of money and accounts every month to meet every bill, but that didn't mean it wasn't stressful.

'Would you like a drink first?' she asked.

'If you do.'

'OK.' She'd felt confident up on the mountain but now she was flustered again. The routine of making the hot drink would calm her nerves, she decided. 'The kitchen's out the back.' She went ahead, put on the kettle and gathered the cups.

She'd meant for him to wait in the living room but he followed her. He pulled out one of the wooden chairs, swung it around and straddled it. The movement drew her eyes to the long strength of his thighs but she looked away hurriedly when she realised where her eyes really wanted to go.

'Do you do this sort of thing often?'

'What?'

'Bring men you barely know back to your home for sex.'

'Ah.' She dropped her head. 'No. Not really.' The water was being painfully slow to boil. She turned around and adjusted the heat under the water to maximum, put a generous spoonful of cocoa in each cup, then turned back to him and met his steady look fixedly. She felt defensive. 'Why? If I said yes, would you lose interest?'

'I'm not judging you.'

'Aren't you?' She wondered. It was a loaded question to ask. Double standards weren't extinct but still it disappointed her that he might harbour them. The water boiled and she used a tea towel to lift the kettle off the heat, then poured their drinks. All the while she avoided his gaze even though she felt it prickling against her face. 'Well, alternatively, what if I said, I haven't had sex in five years? Would that make you more or less interested?'

'What if we stopped playing the sorts of games you've already told me you don't want, and you simply told me the truth?' He took the cup she handed him, murmured his thanks, and held her gaze. 'Or despite your professed desire for honesty, is that idea far too radical this early in our relationship?'

'We don't have a relationship. And that would be pushing the boundaries even if we did, yes.' She checked the date on the carton of milk in the fridge, grimaced, then sniffed it to make sure it hadn't gone off, but then she couldn't bring herself to pass it to him. 'Sorry. I hope you don't mind it without milk.' She returned the carton to her fridge. It would be fine on her cereal in the morning but she'd never forgive herself if he got sick. 'I need to shop.'

'You're not going to tell me then?'

'My private life is my private life. You wouldn't like it if I started questioning you. What if I said, what about you? When's the last time you had sex with a woman you barely knew? Was it yesterday? Or maybe the weekend? Or have you been a good boy this week and was it all of a week ago the last time?'

He put down his drink. He swung himself out of the

chair and came towards her. His smile annoyed her. She hadn't meant to be funny and him finding her so felt as if it gave him control of the conversation. But he leaned into her and nuzzled the side of her cheek and she forgot her irritation as her pulse raced immediately.

'Ask away,' he murmured. 'As long as you're sure you want to hear the answers.'

'I know all I need to know, thank you.' She let her hands play across his chest. She hadn't ever met anyone with shoulders this broad. 'Could you kiss me please?'

'Where?' He touched her chin. 'Here?'

Kelly arched her neck. 'Up a little.'

'Here?' He touched her forehead.

'Down.'

'Here then.' Shockingly, before she could even think what he could be doing, he undid every button on her shirt. Without ceremony he parted the linen, revealing her aching, lace-covered breasts. He studied her for a few seconds and his expression turned oddly taut.

She couldn't breathe. 'Please.'

'You're stunning.'

'Nothing special.' She had one prosaic second of ordinariness when she had time to be grateful for the impulse that had made her wear her very best and most rarely worn underwear that morning – most of her stuff was cotton and plain rather than lacy and sexy and this was all she had that wasn't so well washed it was ragged – but then he shifted and there was nothing in her mind but Jack and what he was doing to her. She felt her head go muzzy even before his mouth reached her and when he kissed the creamy curve above the lace fastening at the front, her legs almost gave way.

'When, Kelly?'

'Mmm?' His mouth crept along the curve and his tongue dipped deep within it and she gasped. Her nipples puckered so hard she felt the tug on her flesh as they tightened. That had never happened before, she'd never felt anything that intense, she'd never even realised her breasts could be that sensitive. She grasped helplessly at his shoulders to prevent herself falling.

'When was the last time?'

'What?' The probing, seeking, secretive movements of his mouth were heavenly but the calm deliberateness of his tone more than the words themselves gradually penetrated the haze surrounding her and she shook her head dazedly and used one hand to lever herself back slightly. 'What did you say?'

He lifted his head. She was flushed and damp and unsettled but aside from a deepening of colour at his cheeks he looked entirely in control. 'I want to know the last time you had sex.'

She dragged in a few steadying breaths. 'It really matters to you? I don't understand. Why?'

'When?' He moved both hands from her waist and cupped her breasts, sending her dizzy again. His thumbs moved against her nipples, and twin shafts of pleasure sizzled along her nerves and she closed her eyes involuntarily, only just managing to stifle a sigh of need.

'Is it so terrible to tell me?' he asked softly, still caressing her. His thumbs touched her nipples again and she felt her damp body moistening further, preparing itself for him. Her body moved, her hips lifted towards him in silent yearning but Jack murmured a soft rebuke and shifted and didn't let her touch him.

She tried to think why it could be terrible to tell him, and couldn't remember. His fingers unfastened her bra and opened it out. His gaze heated, he bent and put his mouth to one nipple. She drew in a quick, shuddering breath with the shock of the pleasure. As long as he kept doing that, Kelly thought desperately, then everything would be all right. 'Almost five years,' she gasped. 'My husband.'

'No one since the divorce.'

'No.' She brought her hands up to hold his head against her when he seemed about to draw back. 'No one. Don't stop.'

But he'd stopped and he resisted her attempts to force him back to her. 'What about the condoms you mentioned?'

'They're from my flat-mate. She gave them to me for my birthday. As a joke. I haven't even opened the box.'

'Yup!' Without warning he dropped his arms and stood up straight and took a step back. She sagged back against the stove behind her, but he murmured something and caught her shoulders and steadied her before she could fall, then released her when she was steady. Expert fingers refastened her bra and then he folded her shirt across her chest. 'That fits the picture I was beginning to put together.'

'Jack?' She stared at him when he moved away from her. 'What are you doing? You're leaving?'

'You got it.' He swung the chair he'd used earlier back beneath the table.

'What does it matter if it's been a while for me? I told you before, I know exactly what I'm doing.'

'Sure you do.' But he was already out the door. 'What about the morning?' he threw back as he moved down the hallway towards the front door. 'Your car's still at Karori. It's too late for you to come all the way out now so I'll drive over first thing and pick you up here.'

Kelly chased him, clutching the sides of her shirt together when they flapped open as she ran. 'I'd rather catch a bus.' Her head was still reeling, this time with dismay more than desire. 'You're really leaving? Why? What did I do wrong?'

'Oh, Sweetheart.' He looked as if he might grin then. 'You did nothing wrong.'

'Then this is silly.' She pursued him to the door but he was too far ahead of her and she couldn't stop him walking out. 'You don't need to do this. If this is some elaborate seduction thing you like to do to build up the tension then trust me, there's no need – ' She broke off at the rebuking look that earned her, but at least he'd stopped at the gate. 'Please. Don't go.'

'Is that really what you think? That this is a seduction trick?' His tone was strangely heavy and now he hesitated. When he started back towards her she went stiff with anticipation and her heart started pounding.

'I don't care what you're doing, I just want you to kiss me,' she whispered.

'I don't do tricks.' He took her face in his hands and stared down at her, his eyes very dark. 'I've never needed to.' He lowered his mouth, plunged his tongue into her mouth with a passion that seemed to match every fraction of her own but then, just as she thought she might die if he stopped, he drew back sharply again. 'This is all real, Kelly.' His gaze was so hot it almost hurt her to return it. 'And when I'm sure you know what you're letting yourself in for, there's no way in the world you're going to be able to hold me off. But I'm going because right now you're too tempting and I'm not used to being self-sacrificing.'

He was outside again before she even realised he was gone. 'It's not like you'll be seducing a virgin,' she hissed, wanting him to hear but not her neighbours. 'Five years might seem like a lifetime to someone like you but it hasn't made my hymen grow back! You don't need to be self-sacrificing.'

He grinned at her then, and shook his head as if to tell her off, but all he said was, 'Sweet dreams,' before he climbed into the Porsche. He lifted an arm in farewell and the car started with a low, throaty growl and within seconds he was gone.

Kelly shut the door carefully then tipped her head back against it and stood there, trembling, long after she heard his car turn out of the street. Sweet dreams, she thought sickly. *Sweet* dreams…? As if!

Eventually, after calling him in her head every impolite name she could think of, she rallied herself. She poured their drinks down the sink, rinsed the cups and left them on the rack to dry, then went down the hall to the bathroom.

She'd had a lucky escape, she tried to tell herself. Bizarrely, his conscience had bothered him and she should be grateful for that. He was too observant, too knowing, and far too compelling. It would be prudent, she knew, to pretend today had never happened.

She undressed and put her hair up.

The safe thing would be to back-flip completely. The safe thing would be to be cool and calm and simply apologise for her forwardness and say she'd changed her mind about what she'd thought she'd wanted. He'd be too sophisticated to question her and the subject would probably never be raised again.

In the mirror above the basin she looked flushed. Her

eyes still glittered with remnants of the excitement he'd roused and her breasts were so swollen and tight they looked unfamiliar. She studied her reflection gravely for a few minutes, then dropped her eyes sharply and turned away to open the door to the shower.

She couldn't remember ever being more profoundly aware of her body and her femininity.

On Thursday morning Jack didn't get close enough to Kelly for any exchange beyond that of looks – his, friendly; hers, anything but – before their ward round. But he could tell from the cold stare he got when she came up to where he and Tania were talking together on Maui at the start of the round that his number was definitely not at the top of her speed-dial list this morning.

He liked that. He wasn't entirely sure of his motivation for leaving when he did but it had felt right at the time and it felt right now. But he liked it that the resulting frustration hadn't been all on his side.

She wore jeans again, cut closer than the ones she'd worn yesterday, meaning that when she bent or crouched to examine or talk with a child in that gentle, special way Kelly had with children, the fabric tightened around her bottom. His breath caught in his throat every time it happened. The loose, green shirt she had on should have been less revealing than the lemon close-cut one she'd worn the day before, because the soft way that had clung to her breasts had left him in a permanent state of discomfort, but paradoxically the looser shirt was just as bad. She had the sleeves rolled up and the neck unbuttoned, and the skin of her throat and neck looked so smooth and creamy that he wanted to put his mouth to the V of her throat and lick her just to check again that she wasn't all ice cream.

Her hair was twisted up today, fastened with a gold clip into a swirl at the top of her head. The triumphant glare his scrutiny of the style earned him, reminded him that he'd told her he preferred it loose, but he smiled back at her. He liked her hair up too, he knew now. With the strands at the top splayed out at every angle the way she'd arranged them, the look was fresh and youthful.

It left him imagining her, warm and soft and yielding, barefoot and naked under one of his shirts, just out of bed on a summery Sunday morning.

Lost in contemplation of that, he looked across with a start when Roger Gleisener addressed him directly.

'Jack, what do you think?' The older man came around beside him. 'Are you with me on this?'

'I'd change, yes,' he agreed steadily. They'd been discussing the antibiotics Kelly had prescribed for her patient's cellulitis, a type of infection under the skin, which in this case had spread from a superficial graze by the child's ear and had made the left side of her face red and angry-looking. The potential was there for rapid spread. The child was allergic to penicillins and the alternative Kelly had given her intravenously for the last twenty-four hours had made little difference. In places the cellulitis was worse and the marker lines Spencer had drawn around the boundaries of the redness on admission had been overrun.

According to the results from the microbiology lab, the bacteria should have been sensitive to the drug, but in practice there'd been no obvious response. 'I'd change this morning then review again at six tonight if there's still no improvement. I'm on call tonight so I'll keep a close eye on things.'

'Thanks.' Kelly nodded and their senior house officer

promptly made the appropriate change on the child's drug chart, then stayed behind when the rest of them moved on to the next bed, to administer the first dose of the antibiotic immediately.

Jack waited for Kelly to walk ahead of him. He knew she'd been looking at him when he'd been talking with Roger but when she saw him there her gaze veered away and her expression turned distant again.

He smiled. He still wasn't altogether sure what was happening between them. But it felt good.

Brett Spinks, his eight-year-old with kidney failure and a chest infection, was considerably brighter. Three days of intensive physical therapy and antibiotics seemed to have turned his infection around.

'He's pretty much cleared his chest now,' the ward's senior physio assured him. 'We've tailed off our work over the last day or so. He's been working hard, haven't you, Brett?'

'I'm going for a ride in Dr Jack's Porsche,' Brett pronounced loudly, and Jack was amused that the child seemed to think he could guarantee that by making sure everyone knew about it. 'My dad's coming too.'

'I didn't say anything about a ride or your dad,' Jack objected. He exchanged amused looks with Brett's mother. 'You're making up stories.' He sat the boy forward and listened to the back of his chest, shushing him when he tried to argue, so that he could hear properly.

'Good. Very good.' He nodded to Brett's mum and to the physio once he'd finished. 'It's clear. Well done. We'll make it Sunday for home, after dialysis. All right with everyone at home?'

'Sunday's great.' Brett's mother nodded enthusiastically. 'We'd like that. He'll be finished dialysis around lunchtime so we'll take him home after that. Thank you.'

Kelly would be on call for the weekend, he knew, and he looked at her deliberately, amused by the determinedly remote look she directed back at him. 'I'll come in Sunday morning and see Brett myself before he goes.'

'Don't forget,' contributed Brett. 'Because of the car.'

'Because of the car,' Jack echoed, looking back at him. 'You know that's going to depend on how much you eat between now and then.'

The ward's nurse manager, Tania, murmured, 'Brett's been very good with his meals. We haven't had to send a single one back in days.'

Brett looked proud and Jack grinned at him. 'Looking good, mate. Keep it up.'

'You couldn't give them all a ride, could you?' Tania asked him as the group moved on to the next side room on the ward. 'If we could promise them that we'd have half the kids on the ward quiet as lambs all day.'

'No one's getting a ride.' Jack rolled his eyes. 'That's a groundless rumour and it's time it was squashed. I haven't said anything about a ride. I promised him ten seconds sitting in the passenger seat, nothing more.'

She laughed. 'You do realise that most of his school friends are coming to see those ten seconds?'

'Now, Tania,' he growled. They were behind the group now and he put his arm around her shoulders and squeezed her warningly. 'I'm making you personally responsible for making sure they know to keep their hands off the metal and tucked away in their pockets. If you don't do your job properly you might see violence in the car park.'

'You're all talk, Jack McEwan,' she teased. 'I know you, you'll be giving them driving lessons in it. I shouldn't have to tell you that that's what they're all expecting.'

He winced. 'Stop! You'll give me nightmares.' They'd caught up with the others now and he hugged her side briefly before releasing her to let her skip ahead and join her nurses.

He smiled then shifted his gaze, saw Kelly, beside Roger, staring at him, and looked back enquiringly. But she turned her head away sharply before he could figure out what was annoying her now.

He was on call all day and for the night. He told Kelly after clinic to go early and that he'd sort out problems on the ward, but predictably she refused to leave until she'd reassured herself about the progress of all her patients and so they did a round together.

'This is better,' she decided, when she examined her young patient with the facial infection after her changed antibiotics. 'I'm happy with this. Are you, Jack?'

'I agree.' It was too soon to expect major changes but the redness outside the pen line Spencer had drawn around the child's cheek had faded and it seemed to be becoming less angry within the boundary. 'Her temperature looks as if it's on its way down,' he commented, passing Kelly the chart.

'We'll review again in the morning,' Kelly concluded. 'I saw a six-year-old in clinic this afternoon with a flare-up of his asthma,' she told him when they stopped at the nursing station after the round to deposit the notes and charts they'd used. 'He improved enough to go home, but his mum's going to bring him in if she's worried about him overnight. He wasn't too bad and I don't think you'll see him but admit him under me if you do. The on-call registrar knows about him and I've told Admissions and given Reception his notes so they'll be there if you need them. Apart from that, no problems on my side.'

She gathered a bundle of journals from the trolley against her chest, then hesitated, and looked briefly at Tania who'd come up and was clearly, but patiently, waiting to speak to him. 'Are you coming for a drink upstairs?'

'No time tonight.' Jack nodded at Tania and signalled to say he'd be only a few seconds. With the further improvement in Cindy's condition over the last twenty-four hours, he realised that he hadn't had a chance to talk with Cindy's parents. So, as soon as he'd sorted out whatever it was Tania wanted, he intended to go to the unit to pass on the good news. 'Another time, Kelly?'

'Sure.' Her eyes swung to the nurse manager and she added haughtily, 'I understand. Maybe you should buy one of those machines they use for controlling queues. That way we could all take a number and wait our turn and there'd be no pushing in.'

Both Jack and Tania stared after her when she stalked off.

Jack said, 'I've missed something.'

Tania, beside him, looked as mystified as he felt. 'I've known Kelly four years and I've never heard her say anything even remotely snappy before. She's the sweetest, most even-tempered, good-natured person I know. She couldn't be...?' She cut off the words. 'No, of course she couldn't be. Not Kelly. That's silly. She's far too sensible.' She smiled. 'I was going to say jealous.'

'Jealous?'

'Of me.' Tania put her hand around his elbow. 'I was going to say, maybe she likes you. I was going to say, she must have heard the rumours about us by now. And she has been on edge with me since yesterday for some reason. But then I remembered that she's only been back this week. So there's no reason she'd mind. Not unless...' She broke off again. 'Jack, you haven't?' Her eyes widened in a shocked way as if she'd seen something in his face he hadn't intended to reveal. 'Not in three days. Not poor Kelly!' she cried. 'How could you...?'

'Shame on you.' Jack turned her around and pushed her away. 'You have a nasty, suspicious mind.'

'I'm sorry.' But the look she sent him was stiff with suspicion. 'It's just that I'm very fond of her. I feel protective. I know she seems very outgoing on the surface but unlike some others round here,' she darted him a quick, laughing look, 'Kelly's a very private person. She's not the sort of woman who'd rush into anything with any man she didn't get to know very well.'

'Don't you think,' Jack said softly, his hand at her back guiding her away but sparing a quick, thoughtful look himself back at the door that still swung heavily from Kelly's violent exit, 'that I can tell that?'

chapter seven

Kelly spent Friday morning in meetings and at clinic in town, and in the afternoon she attended her major Oncology clinic of the week at Wellington Hospital. She didn't normally bother going back to Karori after that session, but today decided she wanted to bring herself up to date with the wards.

There was also a chance Jack would still be at work. Not, of course, that that was the reason she was going.

Which was just as well, since by the time she arrived on Maui ward there was no sign of him. Tania, who'd stayed late to get on top of some of her administrative work, explained he'd left a little while earlier.

'No problem.' Kelly collected up the charts she needed. 'I'll be fine on my own.'

But Tania insisted on joining her and at the end she coaxed Kelly into joining her for coffee even though Kelly, embarrassed about her outburst the day before, had hoped to avoid any tête-à-tête until she'd worked out how best to explain.

She started with an apology but the manager waved her hands and cut her off before she could finish. 'Don't worry about it, I understand,' she said. 'Consider it forgotten.'

Kelly said, 'I don't know what got into me,' and Tania laughed.

'Oh, I have a pretty shrewd idea.' She waggled her eyebrows when Kelly stared at her in shock. 'I've been thinking about this since yesterday, and I finally concluded that you're all grown up. There's no reason why you shouldn't do what you want. So don't listen to the stories, Kelly. You don't have to be jealous of me. I only went out one night for dinner with Jack. Which is no big deal – right?'

'But...but I thought that you and he...'

'Oh, sure, I really like him. In fact, I think he's drop-dead gorgeous, great fun, and the man definitely knows how to make a woman feel attractive. But, that's it as far as I'm concerned.

'What about your husband?'

'It was because of him that I went out that night with Jack. Anthony's girlfriend is nineteen. *Nineteen!* Think about that, Kelly. I'm almost twenty-nine. That's a *decade* more. I've spent the last six months missing him like hell, but hating him too and feeling old and ugly and disgusting and undesirable and sure that no man would ever look at me again.' She gave a heavy sigh

'And then, suddenly Jack arrived to take up his job here in the hospital,' Tania continued. 'He's warm and funny and sexy and I like him. So, when he invited me out for supper, and asked me to show him around the district, we had a great time with lots of laughs. And then, suddenly I feel attractive and happy about myself again. I'll always be grateful to him for giving me back my self-respect.'

Kelly felt ashamed of her earlier unworthy thoughts about Tania and Jack's involvement with one another.

'For heaven's sake, Tania!' she exclaimed. 'Despite what you say, you're obviously still young and you're beautiful. Of course men are going to look at you, and...'

'I forgot that until Jack came along,' the nurse interrupted. 'What happened with my husband, Anthony, blinded me to that. But, when Jack reminded me what it was like to feel like an attractive woman again, he didn't just help me regain my self-respect, he also gave me back my confidence. I called him the other day.'

Kelly looked at her blankly. 'Jack?'

'No – Anthony.' Tania smiled. 'We met Tuesday night. It seems that all is not exactly rosy in his wonderful love nest. The teenager's getting restless. He thinks she's going to do a bunk any day now. He wants to come back to me.'

Kelly gasped. 'Will you let him?'

'I haven't decided.' Tania laughed. 'I'm thinking about it. Probably. Eventually. If he can convince me that he can make me happy again.'

'So Jack means nothing to you now?'

'Not quite nothing.' Tania grinned. 'Let's face it, he's a dreamboat! If, when I was so unhappy and depressed, he'd suddenly announced that he'd fallen madly in love with me, I reckon that there's a good chance I'd have fallen just as hard for him. But, that's nothing but a pure day-dream – a fantasy – and I really don't need that sort of confusion in my life right now. And, if you two get serious about one another, then no one could be happier for you both.'

'Serious isn't in the option list.' Kelly rinsed out her cup, left it on the draining rack and headed for the door. 'I'm *definitely* not interested in "serious"!'

On Saturday morning she rose flushed and thick-headed and not remotely refreshed. A long, cooling shower went some of the way towards waking her up. She was grateful that it was Saturday, so that the traffic was light and the drive to work short. The lingering eroticism of her dreams, along with the memory of the way her new colleague continued to dominate them, had left her distracted and vague, not in the best shape for concentrating on the road.

She spent all morning and the first part of the afternoon in her office dealing with paperwork. The work was mundane and tedious and when her brain gave out around three she drove home and devoted the rest of the day to the garden. In the evening she drove back out to Karori after Spencer rang her to discuss a child he was worried about.

He didn't need her to see the nine-year-old, but Kelly was worried enough to want to for her own peace of mind. The girl had developed painful red lumps on her shins, a symptom sometimes associated with serious illnesses such as tuberculosis. Since the little girl had a cough and chest pain and an abnormal chest X-ray, Spencer felt TB was likely.

Kelly examined Letitia carefully then studied the results of her tests including her X-rays. 'I agree,' she told Spencer slowly. Initial infection with the TB bug rarely caused problems in children in normal health, but a second infection or even reactivation of the old infection could bring on active disease later, and one of those seemed the most likely scenario here.

They couldn't yet be sure how infectious Letitia's TB was, but as a precaution the nurses had swapped beds around on the ward to free up a side room with an independent ventilation system.

Kelly explained to Letitia that she was going to have to wear a surgical mask over her nose and mouth whenever she left the room, as well as when anyone came to see her.

'That looks pretty,' Kelly told her, demonstrating how to put one on. 'I can see you're good with bows. People will think you're one of the nurses when you're wearing this, so you'll have to remind them that you're just a little girl.'

The child smiled. 'They won't think I'm a nurse. I'm too little.'

'You still look like a nurse with it on,' Kelly teased lightly. 'And people are silly sometimes. If you don't watch out they'll have you doing all the work around here.'

'I might be a nurse when I grow up.'

'You should be a doctor,' Kelly suggested. 'We need more lady doctors.'

'I don't know about that.' Spencer grimaced. 'My class in Dunedin was sixty per cent female. Us poor men are being drowned out.'

'You "poor" men?' Kelly laughed. 'Oh, I like that. Don't take any notice of him, Letitia. There are far, far too many men already around here.'

Spencer laughed at the time but the next morning when they finished their ward round, in her office he said in passing, 'I've never thought about it before, but I guess you probably do feel a bit outnumbered around here, Dr West. It can't be easy being the only woman on our side of the team. You probably get a bit lost when we guys talk sports.'

Kelly looked at him sideways. 'That's a very sexist observation,' she pointed out. 'I talk sport when I need to. I suppose you think that if the team was mainly women we'd spend our spare time discussing cooking and cleaning.'

He smiled. 'What I meant to say was that if you're interested in finding someone around here who wants to offer you more than mundane conversation, then look no further.'

She smiled back. 'I'm your consultant,' she reminded him.

'I've always found older women sexy.'

Older...? Kelly sighed. She had four years maximum on the younger doctor, possibly less. Clearly, though, every month showed. 'Don't flirt with me, Spencer.' She tapped her palm twice to the registrar's flushed cheek. 'Or I'll fail you your attachment.'

'Ouch.' He made a mock wince at the threat, but then smiled. 'OK. Sorry. Message received. I'd like to salvage my career now, please.'

'Wise man.'

'If you ever have second thoughts...'

'It won't happen,' she proclaimed. 'Forget it. Now get lost. Leave me in peace to sort out this stuff.' Concentrating on the chart she had out, she waved her arm vaguely at the door and felt him move away. Still smiling, she turned to watch him go, but then she stilled as Jack moved out of the doorway to make room for the younger doctor to leave. The paediatrician's slow grin told her he hadn't missed a thing.

'I'm impressed,' he drawled. 'Handled like an expert.'

'From you, I'll take that as high praise.' She grimaced. 'Have you come to annoy me, or are you a workaholic who can't keep away from the place even on your day off?'

'Maybe I can't keep away from you?' But he smiled again at her flat, disbelieving look. 'I told you I'd see Brett myself,' he went on easily, and she remembered then that he had mentioned that earlier in the week.

She hadn't seen the child yet because he hadn't been on the ward during her round. 'He's in dialysis.'

'He should be about due to finish any time.' He

wandered towards her, pitched himself against the edge of her desk, and eyed the chart she'd been studying. 'Who's this?'

Kelly told him about her new admission.

Letitia's X-rays were on the board and he inspected them. 'You want me to take over, I assume?'

'Please.' Within the team, each specialist generally took over care of patients admitted with illnesses within his or her area of expertise. Jack, as an infectious diseases specialist, would take over Letitia, and if he admitted children with cancer when he was on call then Kelly would look after them in return.

'How about contacts?'

'We'll put in a notification so they'll be traced and checked. The family is in its third generation in New Zealand but they've had relatives staying recently from Samoa so that may be a possible source if this is a new infection.'

'I'll go and see whether Brett's finished dialysis,' Jack said, after their discussion about Letitia finished. 'If I get a chance I'll look around for Spencer as well, make sure he's not suffering too much. Do the empathy bit.'

'Don't you dare.' She glared at him. 'Leave him alone. You'll only make it worse and if he's suffering he deserves it. He's old enough to have known better. Besides, he called me an older woman. He deserves all the grief that's coming to him.'

Jack laughed. 'But then I find you sexy too, and you're definitely not old to me. With your hair like that you could almost pass for a teenager.' She had her hair down in a braid across her shoulder and he picked it up then let it drop against her chest, experimentally, as if testing the weight. 'But you're a hard woman, Kelly West. Poor

Spencer. He doesn't realise that underneath that dazzling smile, beats a heart of cold stone.'

'Granite,' she agreed, flicking her braid over her shoulder away from him when he went to stroke it again. 'I'm untouchable.'

Knowing Jack was around didn't make concentrating on paperwork any easier and she was almost relieved when he came back an hour-and-a-half later. 'Time to take you away from this,' he told her. He'd come straight in without knocking and now he stood behind her and played with her braid again. 'No one should work all Sunday with no break. We'll have lunch. I've checked out Letitia. Her mum tells me she has a four-week-old baby at home, so we're going to have to keep Letitia as an in-patient for three weeks at least, to be doubly sure she's not infectious when she goes home. You must be finished here.'

'The nature of paperwork is that it never finishes. I spent most of yesterday on it too and there's tons left still.' She sighed, then leaned back in her chair and looked up at him from upside down. One of the nurses had just been in to tell her how Jack had spent an hour driving an excited Brett, his equally-excited father, and a dozen or so of Brett's little school friends, in turns around the streets outside the hospital. 'Have they worn you into a nervous wreck?

'Still shaking,' he agreed, with a smile. 'The car's going to have to go in for a full detail in the morning. I was supposed to be playing golf this afternoon but I decided I'd rather spend the time with you, so I called up someone to substitute for me. So let's go, hmm? Come back to this after lunch.'

'You cancelled golf for me?' Her pulse bumped a little in her chest and she fluttered her lashes up at him deliberately. 'I'm so flattered.'

'You should be.' He leaned over, saved her work and shut down her computer. 'It's a big step in our relationship. Move it.'

Kelly faltered briefly. *Relationship*…? She looked up into his bland expression and decided he was teasing her again. He had to be. From all she'd heard about Jack, he clearly hadn't a clue about the meaning of the word "relationship".

Meeting his smile then with a deliberately bright, only mildly fazed one of her own, she collected her bag, phone and bleep and followed him out. Things were quiet on the wards and if Spencer needed help or advice he knew how to get hold of her.

'I shouldn't be coming with you,' she told him, following him anyway. 'I eventually decided after Wednesday that I was going to tell you I'd changed my mind about having sex with you, and I only want to be professional colleagues from now on.'

He was behind her and she glanced up at him and saw her words had amused him. 'And what changed it back again?'

'L-u-s-t,' she spelled out lightly. 'I seem to be obsessed. I look at you and my temperature goes up two degrees. I used to think about sex a couple of times a month, now it seems like it's a couple of times a minute. How long do you think that will take to go away once we've slept together?'

'I doubt it'll ever go away.' He slid his arm around her back to guide her out of the stairwell towards the hospital's main entrance. 'I think you're hooked.'

'No I'm not.' Despite the warmth of the afternoon Kelly shivered. 'I'm far too sensible for that.'

'Shall we make that trip to Makara today?'

She dipped her head slightly. 'Why not.'

They bought filled rolls and soft drinks from a dairy on the main street and then turned off towards Makara. The long road down to the beach was narrow and steep in places and passed through green farmland and patches of scenic bush, and she could tell from his grin as he poured the Porsche around a tight bend that he was enjoying the challenge of the route.

'If you crash the car on the next bend and I die, I'd like to be buried here please,' she said pointedly, indicating the cemetery they were just passing. The site spread up the hill, amidst beautiful countryside, with views right out to the coast. 'That way I can spend eternity haunting you every time you frighten some poor driver coming the other way on that corner again.'

'O ye of little faith.' He laughed, but he did, to her relief, slow down slightly.

He parked in the shingle parking area just off the stony beach at the bottom of the road and they wandered down towards the water. It was a warm, sunny afternoon, the tide was out, the air was fresh and salty, gulls were crying above and children were laughing and splashing and fishing in the shallows.

They walked along a little away from the cars and sat away from the rest of the people at the end of the stony shore. Kelly finished her food, took off her trainers and wiggled her toes while Jack lay back and closed his eyes. A while later, when he still didn't open his eyes and his breathing became slow and steady, it occurred to her that he'd fallen asleep. She glared across at him, offended that he could relax and dismiss her closeness so easily, while her awareness of him remained so acute that she tingled.

A panting collie raced past them, then back again, stirring up pebbles and sending them flying into Jack's legs. He moved his head and opened his eyes, giving Kelly the incentive to gather her courage. She opened her bag, fished out her sun block, unscrewed the top of it and squeezed a dollop on to her hands.

He'd closed his eyes again, but she knew he couldn't have fallen back to sleep that fast, so she swivelled around, calmly straddled his thighs with her legs, then moved fractionally higher.

When his lashes flickered open, she smiled. 'In case you burn,' she whispered, bending over him. She dabbed cream on to each of his cheeks, and smoothed it in. 'The sun's strong and you haven't brought a hat.' Her fingers traced the roughened curve of his chin then lowered to his throat and the unbuttoned collar of his shirt. She rubbed the block all over. 'Nice?'

'Very nice.'

She rocked forward, deliberately centring herself over him before lowering on to him again. His green-yellow gaze turned suddenly intense, and her own lashes came down and her creamy fingers faltered slightly on his skin as she felt the way he'd already reacted to her. 'I think so too. Mmm. I like this.'

'You're very daring.' His hands came up to grasp her hips and he held her hard against him. 'Feel safe on a public beach, do you?'

'It's just I can't resist you.' She undid the second button on his shirt, then the third. 'You feel nice.' She spread her hand across his smooth, warm chest. 'But you're hot,' she teased, tightening her thighs. 'You're sweating.' His skin was growing damp beneath her hand. 'Best take off this shirt.'

'Best...not.' He levered himself out from under her and moved behind her. With a knowing smile he rubbed his palms over hers to collect the remains of the cream clinging to her then squeezed more of the lotion out of the tube.

'I don't burn,' she murmured, when he touched her face. She rarely went into the sun deliberately these days but although her skin and hair were fair, she'd always tanned well when she was younger.

'Funny.' His fingers rubbed her temples. 'Feels like you're burning up to me.'

When she flushed he smiled and shifted behind her, so her back was against his chest and her legs came in front, inside his. 'Close your eyes,' he soothed. 'Relax. Go to sleep if you like.'

Kelly was more likely to eat a cockroach than to relax at that moment, but she let her head rest back against his chest and gave herself up to the sensual enjoyment of his touch. He massaged the cream into her forehead, her nose and her chin and then her cheeks and her ears and lower to the semi-circle of skin exposed by the rounded neck of her T-shirt.

He squeezed out more cream, then lifted her arms and slowly massaged them below her short sleeves. He lingered on her hands. 'Your skin is incredible,' he murmured. 'All soft and buttery like cream.' He turned her palms over and rubbed them one at a time, then held them up to his face. 'You're going to have a long, happy life, and you're going to fall passionately in love with a nice man who has dark hair and hazel eyes and a very, very nice car.'

She smiled and wiggled her fingers. 'Ah, but do I fall in love with the man or the car?'

Jack sighed. He kissed her ear and she felt his fingers trace her palm again. 'It doesn't say,' he complained.

'Actually I'm not interested in love,' she warned. 'In fact if I thought I was falling in love with you, I'd be running away like crazy right now.'

'Is love so terrifying?'

'No, but you are.'

'Don't you trust me?'

'Not in the slightest.' She moved her head against his chest. 'But that doesn't matter because you can't hurt me. I'm immune to playboys.' He rubbed cream into her throat again and she sighed. 'Mmm, that's nice. If you've nothing better to do this afternoon, I wouldn't say no to an hour or two between some sheets.'

'I love it when you're subtle.' He bit the lobe of her right ear and helped himself to more cream. 'Aren't you even the slightest bit worried that your determination to treat me like a sex object is going to do damage to my ego?'

'Your ego's already the size of a planet. It doesn't need help from me.' She sighed with pleasure as his hands returned to her throat. 'I don't think,' she said a little more raggedly, her eyes flying open and her knees coming up automatically when his fingers strayed inside the neck of her T-shirt, 'I'm in danger of burning there.'

'You can never be too careful.' He folded his left arm across her knees in front of her chest and she realised that even if there'd been people near them they couldn't have seen what he was doing. 'UV can penetrate white cotton.'

'I didn't know that.' She closed her eyes again. Her body felt languid and heavy and when his hand slid into her bra and across to completely cup her breast, she quivered.

He kissed the side of her cheek, and her throat, his mouth warm and seeking, echoing the gentle way he caressed her breast.

'That feels heavenly,' she told him huskily. 'But that doesn't mean you should be doing it in public.'

'No one can see.'

She sighed. Since, after all, this was what she craved, she let her head drop back against him again and concentrated on trying to keep breathing while he slowly, tenderly, caressed her and teased her nipple with his thumb and his palm. It was outrageous, she knew. Sitting on a beach in the middle of the day letting a man, a man she hadn't even known a week yet, fondle her breast, was utterly outrageous. But if felt wonderful and she didn't want him to stop.

When she was almost dazed with pleasure, his tongue touched her ear and then he kissed the right side of her throat and touched his tongue to her ear again.

'How about we go back to your place for an hour or two?'

But he smiled against her cheek and kissed her ear again and didn't move. 'Don't you know, suffering a little first makes it so much better when you do it?'

'I'm already suffering like mad.' Her eyelids felt too heavy to lift. 'My legs won't stop shaking.'

'That's just the beginning.' He kissed her cheek again. 'You taste delicious. One day soon I'm going to be forced to lick every luscious centimetre of you.'

It took ages for Kelly to realise the musical chimes she heard suddenly weren't part of the fantasy she was lost in. When Jack calmly slid his hand out from her top and retrieved the telephone from her bag she almost hissed with frustration.

He opened the phone and passed it to her and Kelly dragged in a ragged breath. 'Hello?'

Expecting it to be Spencer calling about a problem at the hospital, she was surprised when it was her flatmate instead. Geraldine was in a flap because the man from the television rental shop had come around to try and take away her television and VCR. 'He says we haven't paid the rent in three months!' she wailed. 'But I'm sure I gave you the money months ago.'

'You did. And I'm sure I paid it into the account.' Kelly felt ill. She rocked on to her knees, away from Jack, and tried to think. 'In fact I definitely did,' she repeated faintly. 'I didn't have enough cash to pay my share before I went up to Auckland, but I definitely paid the bill the following week,' she remembered out loud. 'The day before it was due.' She'd paid several bills at the same time, the day her holiday pay from the hospital had been credited to her account. 'I paid in person, directly into one of their branches in downtown Auckland. Geraldine, look in the bottom drawer in my filing cabinet, under T for television. There should be a receipt.'

She curled her fist into her hair and avoided looking at Jack while she waited for her flatmate to come back. Kelly rarely had time to watch TV herself. She'd never read the manual to work out how to use the video recorder and if there'd only been her to consider she wouldn't have bothered renting either, but Geraldine was a Coronation Street junkie and she had to tape any episodes she couldn't watch.

'You were right,' Geraldine said breathlessly, a few minutes later. 'It's here, I've got it. He says, sorry for the trouble. There must have been a mistake with the Auckland end not adjusting our account.'

'Thank goodness.' Kelly felt herself relax. She sagged back on to her knees. 'Put him on, and I'll give him the money for the next two months now to save anything like this happening again. It's due soon again anyway.' She reached around for her bag and found her wallet and the card that she usually kept only, since its interest rates were high enough to give her nightmares, for absolute emergencies.

The man sounded gruffly apologetic for the mistake. 'Sorry again, Mrs West. Thanks for being understanding. They need to get their act together up there. It's all computerised, you wouldn't think there'd be a problem.'

'It's not your fault,' she reassured him, before reading out the numbers on her card so he could register the details, along with the card's expiry date.

At the end of the conversation, she folded up the telephone and put that and her wallet back into her bag then schooled her expression and turned around to where Jack watched her speculatively. 'It was all a mistake,' she explained, with a bright smile. 'They thought we hadn't paid the television rental.'

But instead of an understanding smile back, he looked at her steadily, his expression serious. 'Kelly, what's going on?'

She frowned. 'What do you mean?'

'You have a full-time consultant job, you have a private list, you do locums in kids and general practice every weekend you can, plus sometimes even during the week. You use your holidays and Christmas breaks to take on extra work. As far as I can tell you have to be making serious money, yet you have nothing to show for it.'

'I told you, that conversation was a mistake.' But she felt herself pale. 'Where'd you get all that information?

Have you been asking questions about me? Of course I have things. I have a car...'

'A car that should have seen a scrap-heap a decade ago, you share a small, rented flat, you say you hardly ever go out so it's not the high life you're splurging on, yet you still have trouble paying basic bills. None of it adds up. Unless...' He looked thoughtful and pained at the same time. 'Do you have a gambling problem?'

chapter eight

A gambling problem? Kelly blinked a few times. 'I don't gamble. I bought a Lotto Lucky Dip on a whim once but everyone's done that. I've never played cards or…'

'Then where's the money going?'

She closed her mouth. She checked her watch, and scrambled to her feet, slapping down the back of her jeans to try and get rid of the traces of sand and salt that still clung to them. 'It's late. We'll get burnt for real if we stay out any longer.'

He stood up beside her and caught at her hand. 'Talk to me, Kelly. Trust me. Perhaps I can help you.'

'I don't need help.' She pulled her hand away and crouched again, rubbed down her feet and pulled her running shoes back on.

'Sounds to me like you need a whole lot of it.' His tone was cool. 'Do you need cash in a hurry? Give me time to liquidate some investments and I'll give you all you need. Pay me back when you can. I can spare it.'

'Could we leave this please?' The conversation was making her acutely uncomfortable and she was aware of herself flushing angrily as she came back to her feet after tying her laces. 'I don't want your money.' She was used to dealing with her own problems in her own way and she intended keeping it that way. It annoyed her that he thought a few kisses gave him the right to make grand assumptions about her.

The thought that he no doubt expected her to collapse

against him and weep on his manly shoulder and confide her troubles doubly annoyed her. She was an independent woman, totally in control of her own life. She was fully prepared to collapse against him any time he wanted, but not for reasons of handing over her worries.

She'd relied on a man once. She'd stupidly trusted one to take care of her. And look where she'd ended up!

She collected her bag, plus the paper bags and bottles left over from their lunch. 'I'm leaving now.'

She stalked off, her feet crunching on the stones, half expecting to have to hitch back to the hospital. But he followed her. He stopped to talk to a group of teenagers who'd gathered to admire the Porsche, then reached her as she was scuffing her runners beside it. 'You're asking for trouble coming to the beach in this,' she said defensively when he looked at her feet. 'I'm doing my best.'

His mouth tightened. 'I don't care if you get sand in it,' he said impatiently. He unlocked her door and thrust it open. 'It's only a car.'

'If anything that's worth the gross domestic product of a small, third-world country can be called *only* a car,' she muttered under her breath.

'What?'

'Nothing.' He was still waiting for her to climb in and so she did.

'You said something.'

'Nothing important.' She avoided his stony regard and busied herself putting on her seat belt.

Eventually he slammed her door. 'You definitely said something,' he said tersely when he came round to the driver's seat.

'Nothing that should bother you unless the term *conspicuous consumption* pricks your conscience.' She stared straight ahead. 'Which it obviously doesn't.'

He made a harsh sound. 'You're the one who can't pay your bills, yet suddenly I'm the one with the problem?'

'You're the only one who thinks there's a problem.' She folded her arms. 'And for the last time, that call was a mistake. I had paid. I always, *always* pay my bills.'

'You told your flatmate that you had to wait until you were in Auckland to be able to afford that one.'

'It's rude to eavesdrop,' she informed him stiffly. 'And delightful as it is sitting with you here amidst such ostentatious luxury, I'd prefer we moved on.'

His expression hardened. 'Talk to me.'

'I'd rather find another lift.' Kelly went for the door lever, but he reached across and stopped her, imprisoning her against the back of her seat. With a sigh of annoyance, she dropped her hand and gave up.

'I thought we were friends,' he said resignedly.

'We're not friends.' He was so close she could see tiny yellow streaks like spokes in a wheel radiating out through the green of his eyes. He had the same pattern in both eyes, she realised, her gaze switching between the two. Exactly the same pattern. It explained why his eyes often seemed like a mixture of the colours. 'I hardly know you. None of my real friends would be rude enough to pry into my lifestyle and finances. You and I are colleagues.'

He drew back. 'I just spent an hour with a hand inside your T-shirt,' he reminded her curtly. 'Not that I'm complaining, but it's an odd way of relating to a colleague. I assumed we had something special here, or is getting to touch you up a standard perk of the job? If it is, Roger should have told me at my interview. He could have saved the hospital a fortune. I'd have taken the job at half the salary.'

'There's no need to be sarcastic,' she retorted sharply. 'And my wanting to sleep with you doesn't automatically make you special, or a friend.'

His eyes burned into hers. 'So you still want sex?'

Her heart thudded, but she tilted up her chin defensively. 'After such tender foreplay, what woman could resist?'

'Fine.' He jerked away from her, started the car and performed a fast, stone-spinning take off. 'Why should I have reservations, when you so clearly have none?'

Kelly clamped her mouth down hard to stop any remark about the road being far too narrow for the speed he was taking it at. She folded her arms and stared straight ahead all the way back to Karori and his townhouse. She slid out of the car without waiting for him, went ahead up the path and when he came behind her and opened the door, she walked straight inside.

Jack didn't look as if he'd settled in yet. He probably hadn't had time, she decided coldly. No doubt he was out every night. There were unopened tea chests in the first room on the right and a couple more were stacked in the hall. The furniture was standard hospital issue and the only personal possessions on display were the stacks of medical journals on the floor in the main room, the laptop computer and the pile of music discs on the dining table.

She made for the stairs, but before she reached the second Jack put his arm around her and hauled her back roughly. 'Not so fast,' he growled, when she struggled. 'First talk.'

'There's nothing to talk about.' Kelly dipped her head deliberately and bit into the arm he held across her chest, then took advantage of the slackening of his grip to turn around to him. His hands went to her hair to hold her still but, wanting to avoid any more of his awkward questions, she undid as many shirt buttons as she could in a few seconds and pressed her face to his chest and rubbed her mouth against him.

She felt the low, gratifying rumble of his groan against her mouth. His hands shifted restlessly in her hair and grasped her. She felt his response and smiled. He moved from simply restraining her to working at her braid.

She lowered her own hands to his belt, and the hard flesh behind the fastening of his jeans. She found his zip, started to lower it, and felt her hair fall loose around her shoulders at the same time as his hands tangled in it. He grasped handfuls of it and used them to haul her closer.

'Kiss me,' she commanded.

'I'm going to do a hell of a lot more than that,' he bit out roughly against her hair. He put his hands under her buttocks and lifted her. She laughed and put her mouth against his and kissed him, turning dizzy as he returned the embrace with a passion light-years beyond the slow, seductive way he'd kissed her at the lookout on Mount Victoria.

She felt him move towards the stairs but she protested brokenly about how far it was and instead he turned and carried her to the closest surface, sending his discs and books flying as he cleared space for her with one sweep of his arm. He tipped her back and Kelly went willingly, her hair spreading like a gold curtain above and around her, falling off the edges of the table either side of them.

She was still dressed but she spread her legs and held out her arms. He braced his arms either side of her chest, his face flushing, his eyes like hard, green fire. He lowered his body slowly on to hers, but then his expression stiffened, and he stopped, his mouth only centimetres away from hers.

'Now tell me,' he ordered, 'about the money.'

'I have a savings programme.' Kelly dug her fingers into broad, hard shoulders. 'So I can buy my own Porsche.' She arched up from the table but he shifted his head back and she couldn't reach it. He caught her hands in one of his and held them clasped above her head. 'In a decade or three,' she added rebelliously.

'Good story.' He smiled. With his spare hand he caressed her breast through her clothes. His thumb probed her tightened nipple and she closed her eyes and caught her breath at the ecstasy of the sensation, but then he stopped again. 'Choose another one.'

Her lashes fluttered open. 'Is this what you do with all your women?' she asked weakly. 'Torture them until you know everything about them? Did you do this to Veronica? You must be exhausted if you go through this every time. What is it with you and your women? Do you *always* have to be the one who's in control?'

His eyes darkened and she knew then that she had him. 'Do you like it when we spill out all our troubles?' she demanded. 'Does it make you feel powerful and masterly? Is that what turns you on?'

'You turn me on.' But in a single, smooth movement he released her and drew back. 'But that doesn't make my brain shut off and I want to understand why you're doing this.' He gestured at her where she lay still waiting for him, at the table. 'Is this truly how you want it, Kelly? Fast and raw on a table? Is that what brought you here?'

'It sounded pretty good a minute or so ago.' Kelly was already hot but she felt her skin flush red. She looked down at herself, at the table, at her legs, and realised, abruptly, how sordid it must seem. 'But then that was when I thought you wanted the same thing.' She straightened her legs, closed them, and slid off the table. 'Sorry. We could go upstairs. What a bed lacks in spontaneity it makes up for in comfort.'

He ran a hand through his hair, leaving it standing up at the front in a way that made her want to smooth it, but when she lifted her hand he caught it and gave it back to her. He didn't say anything, he just stood there waiting. But she didn't know what she was supposed to say and finally, humiliated, she turned round and walked to the breakfast bar dividing the kitchen from the living area. She braced her elbows and lower arms on it and lowered her head.

'Not again,' she groaned. 'Don't you dare tell me you're too moral for casual sex or one night stands,' she warned him, her voice low. 'That would be a lie and we both know it.'

'I'm not saying I haven't ever had those sorts of experiences.'

'But you're not interested in that with me,' she finished for him. She tipped her forehead forward right on to the bar. 'You never meant to go through with it, did you? You didn't bring me back here to make love to me, you brought me here to make me tell you about the money. You're intrigued. You think there's some mystery and like a typical man you feel compelled to solve it.'

'So trust me and tell me.'

'It's nothing to do with trust.' She sighed. 'This is so silly.' She turned round to face him, bracing her hands behind her across the bar. 'And it's none of your business. There's no need for angst about this. It's simple. You excite me and it's a long time since any man has been able to do that. Because of how long it's been, I may seem overly eager, and if so then I apologise. I didn't mean to throw myself at you the way I have, but – blame frustration. Apart from that, the time thing's not an issue for me. If I'd known that hearing I've been celibate a few years would turn you all sensitive and concerned, I wouldn't have told you.'

'I would have been concerned regardless. You don't add up.'

She sighed. 'I don't know what to do about that. Tell me what works for you, and if it's not too demeaning I'll do my best. Do you like women to prostrate themselves submissively at your feet? Is it abject adoration you crave? Or are you usually content with a few breathless if insincere declarations of undying love and devotion?'

He sat on the edge of the table, the smooth movement drawing her reluctant but compulsive attention to the powerful spread of his thighs. 'I want you, Kelly. Too much to accept a caricature of what you think I want. And too much to let you use me as a convenient whipping boy while you exorcise whatever hurt it is your husband inflicted on you.'

Shocked, she dug her nails on to the laminate surface of the bar. 'That's absurd – '

'No it's not. You're like a hedgehog covered in spines but all soft and squishy underneath. You're putting on an act, and before this goes any further I want to know why.'

'There's no act,' she insisted. 'I have gone out of my way to be honest with you.'

'Nothing about this afternoon's been honest. The way it looks to me, this cynicism you're cultivating is either your way of getting back at your ex personally, or your way of punishing men in general. Is using me like some mechanical stud your way of gaining control again? Or is it much simpler than that? Do I just frighten you so much that this is the only way you can deal with it?'

'You don't frighten me,' she retorted sharply, letting her tone grow angry lest he sense how thoroughly he'd disturbed her. 'I'm not frightened,' she said again, although it wasn't entirely true. 'I find you attractive, and I'm curious to find out if you really are as good in bed as all the rumours say you are. But I also find you slightly pathetic. Any man who's still stuck in the fast cars and sleeping-around stage of male development at your age has to be lacking something.'

She'd intended to cut, to wound and draw blood, but instead he looked thoughtful for a few seconds and then he grinned, and when she flushed with frustrated fury, he laughed at her. He eased himself off his table and came towards her, still laughing, and kissed her forehead. 'You're a perceptive woman,' he said teasingly. 'Apply that gift to your own life and who knows what'll happen. But now it's time for you to go back to work.'

'Is the problem me? Am I so unattractive to you that you can't stay aroused?'

He grinned. 'Sweetheart, I am aroused. I look at you and I'm aroused. I can't remember the last time a woman could excite me the way you do. Being around you at work this week has been hell.' He took her hand and guided it to himself and proved it to her powerfully, but when she went to curl her fingers around him he made a rough sound and lifted her back. 'No way,' he chided.

'What do want then?' she wailed.

'You.'

Kelly rolled her eyes. Sure. That's why he couldn't stop himself making love to her. That's why he was throwing her out. 'I find you extremely aggravating.'

'That's a step up from curious.' He kissed her nose. 'I'll work with that.'

'To what end?' she asked silkily. 'Seduction?'

'There's no challenge in that.' He shooed her towards the door. 'I've decided to marry you.'

'Yeah, right.' Kelly almost swallowed her tongue. 'Good joke,' she choked.

'Glad you like it.' He smiled again then closed the door on her.

Next morning on the round Jack formally took over the care of Letitia. 'She's had another set of blood tests and samples this morning,' Kelly told him.

'Thanks. I'll review her now.' He nodded briskly, his acknowledgement impersonal.

Although Kelly knew he could be simply taking care while they were surrounded by witnesses on the ward round, she felt irritated again that he clearly found it so easy to put aside emotion. She, on the other hand, was still finding it difficult to even think when he was in the same room.

She had to pull herself together, she knew. Having to be around Jack wasn't a passing thing. Unless he grew too bored with New Zealand or Karori to stay, he'd be here, every day when she came to work, possibly for three years, perhaps even longer. Unless she was prepared to give up a very good job, then whatever happened between them, she had to learn to put up with him and anything he decided to throw her way.

But instead of fear, the idea provoked a sharp sense of excitement in the centre of her chest, and she jerked her eyes away from him, half-appalled, half-exhilarated.

On Tuesday she met Sarah and Margie for lunch. Before she could even put her juice and muffin on the table, Sarah pressed her for news about Jack.

Kelly's mind went blank. She sat down carefully and looked at her food and still couldn't think of anything to say. Thankfully it didn't seem to matter because Sarah simply burbled on about how she'd gone to the Golf Club on Sunday evening to meet her husband, who'd spent most of the day on the course. Kelly straightened up when Sarah mentioned that Jack had been there, and when she went on to say that Donna Ling, the young doctor he'd been talking to at the meeting they'd gone to together, had been draped all over him, Kelly stared at her.

'Jack must have invited her to the club because I've never seen her there before,' Sarah went on.

Remembering the way the registrar had shamelessly written her phone number across his hand in town on Wednesday, and remembering too the way Jack had dodged her question about whether he was planning to go out with the younger woman, Kelly believed it.

It shouldn't have hurt. It wasn't as if she didn't know what he was like. And it wasn't any of her business what he did. Why should it bother her if, after caressing her and almost making love to her in the afternoon, he'd spent the night with another woman?

She should be relieved, she told herself. She broke off some of her muffin, lifted it to her mouth, then put it back on to her plate without eating it. She should definitely be relieved. The revelation merely gave her more proof, not that she hadn't already accrued enough, that Jack was exactly the same sort of man as her ex-husband.

'I didn't know there was dancing at the club on Sundays.'

Sarah said, 'They occasionally have a band. It's mostly Saturday, you're right, but it's not unusual to have one Sunday too. They weren't bad. What did you think, Margie?'

'I thought they were very good.' Margie, Kelly saw when she glanced up, was looking at her worriedly and she realised that, unlike Sarah, she probably wasn't oblivious to her shock. 'Mostly they played old disco hits,' the other doctor went on. 'It wasn't close dancing. I don't think Jack seemed particularly happy with the way Donna was acting. I think he was embarrassed. And he left early.'

'But Donna,' Sarah chimed in, with a smile, 'left thirty seconds later.'

'In her own car,' Margie added gently.

'I'm sure he gave her directions.' Sarah's eyes sparkled at them as she sucked soft drink up through a straw. 'What do you think, Kelly?'

'Who knows?' Kelly, still having trouble with her brain, took some of her own drink to buy time. 'Anything could have happened. We all know the man's not exactly discriminating.'

The comment deserved the sharp look she earned from Margie, she accepted, especially considering she knew, after her own experience, that it wasn't true. With her, he'd proved to be *quite* discriminating.

She promptly felt ashamed of herself, but Sarah's delighted whoop made her feel even worse. 'Miaow!' the other woman accused laughingly. 'That's not like you, Kelly. What's the poor girl done to deserve that?' She drained her soft drink, and when Kelly didn't answer, she beamed. 'Or was that meant for Jack? Oh, you're kidding. Don't tell me you've actually...'

'I haven't,' Kelly interrupted smartly before she could

finish. 'I was making conversation. Margie, how's Wendyl doing?' Roger had admitted one of her old patients, a child with severe asthma, to ICU overnight. 'Have you seen him this morning?'

Margie nodded immediately. 'He's much better. We're thinking of transferring him back to you...'

'Speaking of our conversation, look who's paying for a sandwich!' Sarah slapped the back of her hand against Kelly's bare arm, interrupting Margie. 'Oops, he's seen us. He's coming this way.' She tapped Kelly's arm again. 'Look! Wow. Wow! He's so dark and big and...mmm, sexy. I don't know how you can concentrate, working all day with him, Kelly.'

'It's not all day,' Kelly mumbled, carefully studying the crumpled remains of her muffin. 'We're not together every minute.' And she'd given up trying to concentrate around him. She didn't need to look to see he was coming, hidden antennae in her skin had already picked up his presence and brought her out in goosebumps.

'Hi, Margie.' Jack stopped at their table and smiled at them. 'Afternoon, Sarah. Kelly. Good to see you all enjoying yourselves.'

Kelly kept her fixed smile, Margie returned his greeting and Sarah beamed at him. 'Good to see you too, Jack,' she said brightly. 'We were telling Kelly about the band at the golf club Sunday night. The poor girl doesn't get out much. She's practically a hermit most of the time. She needs more of a social life. Perhaps you'll take pity on her and persuade her to come along with you one night?'

'Kelly's not the disco type, Sarah.' He came behind her and Kelly, rigid in her chair, felt him brace his hands on the back of her chair then kiss the top of her head. 'No, you prefer romantic restaurants, long drives and lazy afternoons at the beach, don't you, Sweetheart?'

Beside her, Sarah squeaked but Kelly had turned cold. She jerked her head up but Jack merely smiled blandly then, to her horror, stroked her arms and bent and pressed his mouth calmly to her cheek. 'See you on the ward soon,' he murmured, against her ear but not so quietly the other women wouldn't have heard what he said. 'Don't be long, I miss you when you're not there.'

His departure left a thick silence. Sarah, Kelly was vaguely aware, started to say something, but there was a thud under the table and her friend jumped suddenly, her mouth snapping shut with a click.

She looked up in time to catch Margie eyeing Sarah meaningfully. Sarah shut then opened her mouth again like a fish and then closed it firmly once more. Margie said, 'As I was saying before, Kelly, about Wendyl, we're thinking about sending him back to the wards tomorrow morning.'

'Oh, good.' Kelly's voice sounded unnatural, she knew, but she couldn't help that.

'How's your little girl with possible tuberculosis?'

'The lab and her skin test both confirm it's definitely TB,' Kelly told her. 'Jack's taken over her care and he's started treatment. She'll need to be on the ward three or four weeks because she has a baby sister at home and Jack doesn't want to risk exposing her to it. Em – ' She looked at both women. 'Sorry about that,' she said faintly. 'About Jack before. About what he said, about that kiss – hug – thing. He has a very,' she remembered his comment about marrying her, '*bizarre* sense of humour.'

'I thought it was sweet,' Margie remarked. 'He was defending you from Sarah.'

Sarah looked horrified. 'But I was only joking!'

'We know you were.' Kelly managed a reassuring smile. 'Jack might not have realised, but we do. Margie's teasing.' She looked at her watch, and then her crumpled muffin, and then picked up her plate and juice container. 'I'd better get back,' she decided out loud.

Her brain still felt hazy. She felt as if Jack touching her head had sucked everything sane and rational and sensible out of her skull and replaced it with wool.

They needed to sleep together, she told herself strongly, concentrating fiercely and trying to get her head to start working as she walked out of the canteen. She needed to put Donna Ling and the image of Jack making love to her completely out of her head, and then she needed to persuade him to stop teasing her and to take her to bed. She had to get this distracting sex-craving, desire thing out of her blood, because that was the only way she was ever going to get her life back to normal again.

chapter nine

Jack discharged Letitia at the end of her third week in hospital. He arranged for the family GP's nurse to supervise her anti-TB medication daily at first to be sure she continued her course, then twice weekly once he reduced the regime from the three drugs she was now taking to two. He'd follow her up in his clinic.

As to the rest of his patients, the mild winter and warm spring had made it a bad summer for allergies and asthma, and they'd had to open two of the beds normally designated as winter overflow beds. But work was under control.

He wished he could say the same for Kelly.

He stared out of his window at the Obstetrics and Gynaecology wing, listening to his brother who'd come to discuss arrangements for their parents' fortieth wedding anniversary party at the farm that weekend.

'Tessa, Thomas and I will drop the cakes off with you tonight,' Nathan went on. 'You're sure you're going to have room with all the other supplies you're carting? There's not a lot of space in the front of the Porsche. Tessa can take hers up if there's a problem. Zoe's wreck is off the road again,' he went on, referring to their sister's old Morris Minor, a fond member of the family, but becoming a joke now as extreme age and their sister's shocking driving habits steadily took their toll on the sturdy vehicle. 'The latest boyfriend's a Harley fan and they're coming up on his bike so she's useless as far as transporting supplies goes.'

'There's plenty of room for the cakes on the passenger's side,' said Jack. 'I met Zoe's latest at the weekend.' They'd gone surfing. The waves had been up and they'd spent half a day dodging rocks in the chilling water off Lyall Bay on Wellington's southern coast. 'I like him.'

'Considering Zoe's started going through men the same way you've always gone through women,' Nathan observed with some exasperation, 'you'll probably never see him again after the weekend. Jack, seriously about these cakes. Tessa's worried about them. She's gone to a lot of trouble with them, I'd hate to see them damaged. There are three big ones. I realise they might be damaged if you store them up front but if you stick them on the passenger's seat, where will your date sit?'

Jack frowned as below him Kelly emerged, as he was irritably aware he'd been waiting for her to do, from the other wing. She normally worked in town on Fridays but today she was scheduled for an out-of-town afternoon clinic at one of the region's outlying hospitals and she'd come out to Karori for the morning. She'd been on the postnatal wards checking the infants born the day before.

A woman wheeling a pushchair bearing what looked like about a three-month-old was coming the other way and he watched Kelly stop and hold the door open for them. They exchanged words and he saw Kelly bend towards the chair to look at the child. She must have said something because the woman, looking proud, laughed and lifted out the child and passed her to Kelly to hold.

Jack saw the softening of Kelly's face and the gentle curve of her smile as she cuddled the child. The baby stuck out a hand to touch her face. Through the open window the sound of Kelly's laughter drifted up to him.

'I don't have a date,' he said absently, to Nathan. Kelly handed the baby back and she and the women separated, and he watched Kelly waving back at the pair as she walked off.

'What? You're kidding.'

'About not having a date? Nope.' Kelly was working all weekend.

She'd collected her golden hair in a broad band at the top of her head and it cascaded loose from there and as she moved it bounced against her lower back. He watched, transfixed, when the wind separated the strands and sent them flying behind her in a silken, flaxen cloak.

She disappeared into the hospital's underground car park and he drew back from the window. She was going to her clinic, he knew. She'd be gone all day.

He didn't like knowing he missed her already. He folded his arms and stared down at the path where she'd been. All his adult life when it had come to women he'd always felt that he was the one calling the shots. With Kelly he got a different feeling and he didn't like it. He didn't like it one bit.

It was three weeks since that afternoon at Makara beach when he'd opened his eyes from a half-doze to find her straddling him. She'd laughed and her eyes had sparkled down at him like dazzling blue jewels and her hair had gleamed in a halo of golden sunlight. They'd spent plenty of time together since then, inside and outside of work, yet frustratingly he felt as if he knew no more about her than he'd known that day.

She still had no idea what he wanted from her, he knew. She thought the tension between them would be dissolved with a couple of hours in bed. She seemed sure that by teasing and flirting with him, by brushing him with her hair, or letting her breast or thigh press against him as if by accident, she'd eventually get what she wanted. And all the time she seemed unaware that every bland evasion, every secret, every emotional withdrawal, every refusal to reveal her private self to him, every dismissive sweep of those beautiful blue eyes, needled his pride like a lance flickering into his flesh.

It was time, he decided then, to up the pressure.

'You really have no date? *You*?'

Nathan sounded incredulous, and Jack looked around impatiently. 'It's a family occasion.' Kelly's refusal to spend Saturday with him was doubly frustrating because she wasn't on call for the hospital. She didn't *have* to work, but clearly the GP-run emergency clinic she insisted on covering on her free weekends interested her more than he did. 'What's the big deal?' he asked. 'Why would I bring anyone?'

'Because I've never known you to turn up anywhere without a woman in tow,' Nathan claimed. 'And on a couple of memorable occasions even two. Family anniversaries included. And since we haven't seen you with anyone since that night at the golf club when you had Donna Ling all over you, Tessa and I were starting to think that maybe you were finally taking someone seriously...'

'Don't think.' Jack frowned. 'Nathan, a woman who's had three miscarriages, two late in the first and one early in the second trimester, cause unknown, what are the chances of her ever carrying a pregnancy to term?'

His brother frowned at the change of subject, then said slowly, 'How fully has she been investigated?'

'Don't know for sure, but say fully.'

'As a general rule we say that after three miscarriages

there's around a thirty per cent chance a woman will lose a fourth pregnancy.'

'Which means a seventy-per-cent chance she won't?'

'With the proviso that there's also a higher risk of a complicated pregnancy or premature delivery,' Nathan answered. 'But still if physical and major genetic abnormalities have been excluded, then theoretically, bearing in mind the psychological strain a woman's going to be under, we recommend persisting if she wants children. In more than a third of women with recurrent miscarriages, we never understand the reason. Sometimes time helps. Occasionally changing partners does the trick. I'd have to look at her records to have more idea. Why are you asking this?'

'Changing partners?'

'It may be that the mother's immune system resisted her first partner's sperm, or it may be there was a genetic reason they were unable to produce a viable foetus together. We usually don't discover the answer, but the phenomenon of second marriage pregnancy is recognised.'

Jack nodded curtly. The coffee he'd made for them was cold now but he drained his anyway, crushed the cup and dumped the remains in the plastic-lined bin alongside his desk.

'Send Tessa around alone with the cake tonight,' he commanded. 'It's months since you've let me have any time alone with my gorgeous sister-in-law.'

'Send Tessa alone, like hell,' Nathan countered with a grin as he headed for the door. 'Do I look that stupid? See you around eight.'

'Yep.' Jack lifted his arm in acknowledgement. 'Thanks, Nathan.'

Jack of Hearts 131

He wondered if *he* looked stupid. Was that why Kelly still thought she could handle him?

Kelly was scheduled to be on call that night at Karori, so she drove back there after finishing her clinic. It was a long drive and she was late but Jack had offered to cover for her until her return and she was grateful for that.

She was surprised when the manager of the emergency clinic she normally covered on her free weekends rang soon after she arrived and said that she wouldn't be needed the next two days. 'We've double-booked,' the woman explained. 'Sorry, Kelly. We'll pay you a retainer of course, because we don't want to lose you off the list for next time.'

'How much will that be?' Kelly steeled herself, expecting the sum to be token, meaning that somehow she was going to have to try and find another job at short notice. But the sum the woman named made her gasp. 'That's insane,' she exclaimed. 'You can't be making any money paying that rate without getting anything in return. Are you sure the figure's right?'

'We'll transfer it directly into your account this afternoon,' the woman told her, after assuring her that they valued their staff and there'd been no mistake about the amount. 'Have a nice weekend.'

'I certainly will. Thank you.' Kelly put the telephone down slowly. Jack glanced up enquiringly from the figures they'd been going over – at the next department meeting their team was scheduled to present an audit on length of stay and methods of treatment of infant admissions with croup to Karori – and she stared at him. 'The clinic I cover has cancelled me for tomorrow,' she explained faintly. 'The retainer they want to pay me is only ten dollars less than I earn for the twenty-four hours on duty and twelve hours on call I usually do. Why do I bother working?'

'I don't know. Suppose you tell me.'

She looked down. His ego remained offended, she knew, that she still refused to reveal every tiny detail about her life to him. But that was his problem, not hers.

'We can spend tomorrow together then,' he went on, when she said nothing. 'Since you're free.'

Kelly's pulse accelerated. The nerve-wracking, physical excitement she experienced around him hadn't faded, if anything it grew more exquisite with every disappointment. She'd had a lot of those lately. In the weeks since that fight at his townhouse, apart from stroking her hair and kissing her head or her forehead or her cheek at the end of an evening out, he refused to touch her.

When she made her own advances, frequent, often impassioned advances, he either laughed at her and moved out of reach or held her hands until she gave up. A neurotic person would have a complex by now, she knew.

Lucky she wasn't neurotic.

Much.

'Maybe I could spare a few hours for you in the morning,' she said casually. She picked up her pen and drew a line beneath what she thought was a particularly valid point about shortened stays with continual, rather than intermittent use of humidifiers in enclosed cots. 'In the afternoon I'll have chores to do and a few hours in the garden wouldn't go amiss. What do you want to do? I'm not letting you take me flying.'

'It's way past time you rediscovered your sense of adventure.'

'I've never had one.' She turned the page. 'Except in bed, of course. In bed I have a feeling I could be very, *very* adventurous.'

He made a soft, rough sound under his breath. 'We'll go walking.'

She looked up. 'No climbing. No ropes. None of those karabiner things.'

His eyes turned very green. 'Just walking.'

'Just walking.' She tilted her head and stared hard at him, wondering whether she could believe him. 'If you really, really mean that, then yes. Thank you. I'd love that.'

Danger excited Jack, she'd discovered. Walking for him meant scaling rock faces, and she was scared of heights. Swimming meant surfing, but surf made her think of dumpings and head injuries and filled her with dread. She'd watched him one evening when the waves had been high, and she'd been pale and sick with fear while she'd waited on the beach for him.

'Sunday morning we could do a quick trip down over the Sounds.'

'I told you, no flying.' A friend of Jack's owned a Cessna and since Jack was a keen pilot he'd offered him free use of it. Jack had already tried to persuade her to let him fly her down to the Marlborough Sounds for a sightseeing and wine-tasting weekend. Although she was keen to visit the region one day, she'd been glad that each time he'd asked her, she'd had the excuse of work. The Air New Zealand 737 she normally caught to Auckland made her nervous enough; the thought of being in anything smaller appalled her. Not least because she couldn't imagine flying in a straight line being interesting enough for him, and the thought of mid-air wing wobbles and somersaults terrified her.

'Don't you want to join the mile high club?'

She looked at him then, looked right into two amused green-yellow eyes. 'If I thought you meant it, I might consider it,' she said deliberately. 'But since it's become clear to me that despite your dramatic reputation you're actually completely asexual, I know you're all talk.'

'Tell me you're madly in love with me and I'll make love to you.'

'I'm madly in love with you.'

'Too careless.' His eyes narrowed. 'Think about it more, then tell me seriously.'

But the last thing Kelly was going to do was think about how she really felt. She'd spent weeks carefully focusing on the superficial and the light and on the physical craving she had for him. She wasn't about to risk upsetting anything now by looking at herself any more deeply. So she simply smiled benignly and repeated, obediently, thoughtlessly, 'Seriously, I'm madly in love with you.'

'Tell me your life is worthless without me. Tell me you'll go crazy if you don't marry me.'

'Wrong way round.' She rolled her eyes. 'I'd go crazy if I did.'

His expression darkened at that but she just smiled tauntingly. 'All right,' she said, on a mock sigh, 'If it makes you feel powerful and irresistible, I'll say I'll go crazy – if we don't get this finished tonight.' She laughed and fluttered the paper at him when he eyed her broodingly. 'Come on, Jack. Quit fooling around. Concentrate. Another ten minutes and we'll have it done and then you can go home.'

He lifted a skein of her hair and twined it around his fist. His eyes glittered. 'You think you're in control.'

She didn't think at all. When he looked at her like that

she barely breathed. 'Why do you have to be all-conquering?' she demanded, looking back at her work, lest he saw how he could arouse her simply by looking at her now. 'Why can't my wanting your body be enough?'

'Because delectable as you are, free rein over your body isn't enough for me. I want total and absolute surrender. I want you abandoned and yielding. Mentally and emotionally as well as physically.'

She looked up sharply again, ready to laugh, hoping his expression would still be teasing, but he looked serious. Her smile faded. 'Your ego is out of control.'

'I want you to see someone.' He lifted the handful of hair he still grasped to his face. He closed his eyes as if with bliss, as if touching her hair, inhaling the scent of it, gave him pleasure she could barely imagine, and through her anger she felt her insides liquefy.

Close like this, her senses filled with his warm scent, he made her head spin. 'Your therapist?' she suggested thickly.

'An obstetrician. There's a good chance you can still have children if you're prepared to try.'

'Don't be ridiculous.' Kelly jerked her hair out of his grasp and this time he let her go without protest. 'My fertility, present or absent, has nothing to do with you.'

'I know it won't be easy for you taking a chance again when you've had so much pain in the past, but it's something to think about.'

'How do you know this? How do you know about the chances? Did you talk to someone?'

'Nathan.'

'About me?' she yelped.

'Not by name.' He put one finger across her mouth. 'Will you do it?'

'Of course not.' She was shocked. She drew back from his finger. 'For myself, maybe, I'll see someone, some time.' It was too much to think about now. 'If I'm lucky enough to meet someone nice in the future, someone I know I could trust. I can finish this on my own.' She picked up the papers. 'Go away. I don't need your help.'

'You can trust me. All you have to do is put aside your prejudices.' He slid the work out of her hands before she could stop him. 'I'll finish this,' he countermanded. 'Without *your* help. I'll pick you up at nine tomorrow. Pack swimmers if it's warm.'

Kelly eyed him coolly. 'What makes you think I still want to go to walking with you?'

'Make it eight-thirty then.' He collected his briefcase from behind his desk, shoved the papers into it, then made for the door. 'That gives me plenty of time to persuade you if you're difficult.' When he reached it, he stilled, and looked back at her face.

'I might not be there,' she said defensively.

'You will.' He smiled. 'You're as addicted to me as I am to you, Sweetheart. You won't be able to help yourself.'

It was true. She was addicted to him. But she hated him knowing it and she glared at the door when it closed behind him.

She was ready the next morning when she heard the gate squeak and then banging on her front door. It was cool but according to the radio they were in for a warm day. She wore cropped, cotton pants with a T-shirt and a light jersey now but she had her togs and a towel and a pair of sandals, along with the new sarong Geraldine had just given her as a present, packed in the straw bag she'd slung over her shoulder.

In long shorts and a loose melon-coloured shirt, Jack looked big and handsome and friendly and her heart fluttered at his welcoming grin. When he picked up her ponytail and bounced it over her shoulder affectionately then kissed her cheek, she smiled up at him automatically in return, suddenly light-hearted. They'd been out lots of times during the week but her weekends were mostly taken up with work. This was the first time since that afternoon at Makara that they'd met at all on the weekend, and the morning suddenly stretched ahead like an endless, glorious treat.

'You can't come in.' She put her palms on his chest and pushed. Geraldine was mid-way though highlighting her hair and she didn't want Jack to see her in her foils. She stepped out after him, called out a farewell to her flatmate and pulled the door shut.

'Bossy.' But he took her hand as they went down the path and swung her arm. 'Swimmers in the bag?'

'Yep.' She pushed her sunglasses up on her nose, looked ahead, saw Roger's four-wheel-drive on the street with what looked like *two* boards along with the other stuff on the rack on top, and stopped. 'Jack – ?'

But he laughed at her, and tugged her along. 'Go with the flow, Kelly. I won't let you get hurt.'

'I am not getting on a surfboard.'

'Surf's flat today anyway.'

She had doubts but she allowed herself to be reassured. 'I'm surprised Roger doesn't mind about you borrowing this so much,' she commented, when they started off. 'You've had it at least two nights this week, haven't you? And didn't you go surfing last weekend?'

Jack laughed. 'You're kidding aren't you?' They turned right out of her street and headed down the hill. 'He gets on his knees and begs me to take it. He's so pitiful it's embarrassing.'

'Ah.' Kelly smiled, understanding suddenly. 'He takes the Porsche in exchange.'

He sent her an amused, sideways glance. 'He managed to put far too many kilometres on it last Sunday afternoon.'

'Joy riding to Martinborough,' she revealed. The small town sat in the centre of a flourishing wine region an hour and a half or so from the city. The roads over and back, steep in parts and tightly windy, would have been fun for him, she imagined, in Jack's car. 'He mentioned about two hundred times that he'd been tasting at the weekend.'

Jack rolled his eyes as if in exasperation, but she could tell he wasn't too upset. They chatted easily all the way down into town. When he parked unexpectedly she assumed he wanted to pick up breakfast or lunch. When he steered her into a dive shop, she thought he must need to pick up something for himself.

She lingered on the shelves by the door, looking idly through a discounted basket of swimwear, but after exchanging a few words with someone behind the counter, Jack prodded her into a store-room-cum-changing-room at the rear of the shop.

'Put on your togs,' he instructed, passing her the bag he'd carried for her from Roger's wagon. 'I'll bring you a wet suit.'

'I don't want one.' She went for the door but he held it shut and she couldn't open it.

'Humour me,' he said, through the door. 'Try it on.'

He passed her two neoprene suits a short while later, both with long legs, one black with a single blue V-shaped stripe at the throat and the other blue with yellow markings. The first she tried, the black one, fitted, just, but it was very snug and when Jack, without a knock, walked in and caught her struggling with the zip she glared at him. 'I don't want this.'

He closed the door. 'It's a present.'

'What?' Her head came up sharply. 'Who told you? Has Geraldine been talking to you behind my back?'

'Geraldine?' He looked puzzled. 'I haven't spoken to Geraldine. At least not since I brought you home on Wednesday. What's she supposed to have told me?'

'Nothing.' She swallowed. 'Forget it. It doesn't matter.'

He studied her penetratingly for a few seconds, and she knew she'd irritated him again, but it seemed such a trivial thing to tell him about and so she was relieved when his eyes dropped to her unfastened zip. 'That's a good fit,' he said eventually. 'It's supposed to be that tight. Need a hand?'

'No.' She tugged the zip up to her waist, then higher to below her breasts. 'I'm not buying this. I'll never wear it.'

'You'll wear it with me. When I've turned you into a dare-devil I'll teach you to surf.'

'I don't want to surf.' She was indignant. 'I'll never be daring and I'm scared of waves and I have absolutely no desire to get my head bashed in in a dumping. This is crazy. I'm telling the truth, I'll never wear this again. And you can't buy it for me, it's too expensive.'

'So pay for it yourself.'

As if. She flushed with anger, guessing he knew that she couldn't afford it and wanted her to say it so that he could force more questions on her about why she couldn't, and about what she could be doing with all the money she had to be earning. 'I don't want it,' she said stubbornly. 'I told you, I'll never wear it.'

'And I told you,' he countered, reaching out and lightly tugging at her ponytail, 'you'll need it with me. There is nothing in the world sexier than a woman in a wet suit.'

'You don't look too bad in one yourself.' At the end of the evening when he'd been surfing he'd come up on to the beach, dropped his board and pulled his suit half down to rinse off. The sight of his broad, muscled chest and shoulders above the tight fit of the suit over his hips and thighs had turned her breathless and aching.

Just as she was breathless and aching now.

She jerked her head to shift her hair to the side away from him. 'But what you think I'll need with you is irrelevant. I may never be with you again. This relationship is strictly short-term.'

He smiled. He took her chin and tilted her head slightly, meaning she had to look up at him. 'Still planning to dump me after you've had me, are you?'

'Instantly,' she agreed swiftly. But then she hesitated. She realised she'd avoided thinking that through properly. 'Well maybe after a week or two,' she went on grudgingly. 'Once I've had a chance to get the urge properly out of my system. Then perhaps we'll do it another time later if I get it back again.'

'That's not good enough. I can tell I'm going to have to keep holding out.' He pulled the zip of her top up, his knuckles dragging – deliberately she knew, from the heat that crept up across his throat as he did it – between her breasts, compressing them and making them swell. 'Relax,' he murmured. 'You're all tensed up.'

'You know why that is.' Kelly felt helpless, she was mesmerised like a light-struck possum. 'You can take the tension away. Let's just do it and get it over with.' He had her zip up now to her throat, and his other hand slid

Jack of Hearts 141

outside the tight fabric, slowly over her breasts, her waist, her hips, to settle at the junction between her thighs.

She gasped. Their eyes met and clung. 'Don't stop,' she whispered.

chapter ten

Jack's hand, where it cupped her sex, tightened fractionally. The thickness of the wet suit was between them but still the pressure was devastatingly pleasurable.

'What is this?' he demanded softly. 'What are you saying? Hmm? That you're that desperate that you want it here? Now? Now, with a shop assistant and a bunch of customers on the other side of that door?'

But Kelly was beyond rational thinking. For weeks now her head had been a total mess. Even sleep offered no respite. Everything she needed to get her life back was right in front of her. She bit at her lower lip and reached out to him thoughtlessly, her hand spread, ready to touch, to persuade, but Jack caught her wrist.

His face tightened. One hand still between her legs, the other shifting to her waist, he swivelled her then and rammed her with quiet force against the door. 'Beg.'

'What?'

'You heard me.' He put his mouth to her ear and spoke precisely. 'Beg. I want it all, Sweetheart. I want to hear the words.' He held her with his body, one strong thigh taking the place of his hand, edging between her thighs, separating her and offering pressure exactly where she craved it. He was aroused, she could feel him tight and hard against her, but his body kept her hands contained when she tried to touch him. Although his breathing had sped up his voice was calm with just a slow, raw edge whereas hers was high and broken. 'I want to hear you say it. Tell me how you want me to touch you. Tell me what you want me to do to you.'

'Undress me.' Kelly felt loose. As if she had no bones. It should have been humiliating, she knew, the things he was asking, the way he was encouraging her to move. But it wasn't. She wasn't humiliated. She was unbearably excited. 'Touch my breasts. Let me touch you and kiss you. I want you to come inside me. I want you to make love to me.'

'How?' He put his mouth to her neck. 'Slowly? Gently?' His thigh had hardened between hers and unconsciously her body shifted to take advantage of that. 'How do you want it, Kelly? Tell me.'

'Fast.' She closed her eyes, squeezed them shut, imagining it, feeling him doing it, timing her movements to how she wanted to feel him. 'Hard. No stopping. Take it off.' Her hands, impatient at the barrier between them, clutched at her suit. 'Hurry. Please. I don't want it.'

'I like it. Leave it. Are we doing it, Kelly?' He caught her hands again, stopping her undoing the zip, and then he dropped his hands to her bottom lifting her, effortlessly supporting her weight so she completely straddled his thigh. 'Feel it. Move with it. In your mind are we doing it? Can you imagine it?'

It was as if he was hypnotising her, she thought dazedly, as the images filled her head. 'Yes.' So clearly it was as if it was happening, she realised desperately. Her hips lifted hard, thrust against him. 'Touch me.'

'I don't have to.'

He held her hard, encouraging her, murmuring soft, shocking things directly against her ear and Kelly, helpless to resist the demands of her body, found herself moving uncontrollably.

'Is it good?' He sounded harsher now, as if he'd lost his calm, and his grip at her buttocks tightened and he thrust her lightly against the door.

Kelly couldn't have answered him, her entire world had shut down to the incredible pulsing between her legs but he must have known, he must have been able to tell from the way she looked or the way she breathed because immediately then, when she thought she couldn't bear the tension for one second longer and that she was going to scream out, he covered her mouth with his. His tongue thrust against hers in exactly the same rhythm as her hips were moving and she climaxed immediately.

The world took ages to come back the right way round again. When finally it did, all she wanted to do was hide away in a dark corner somewhere but Jack wouldn't let her go. He stroked her back and kissed her hair and held her trembling body in his arms and then when he saw she'd recovered a little, he kissed her mouth lightly and made her stand up on her own. 'Take it off now,' he instructed calmly. 'We're taking this suit.'

Kelly could hardly argue with that now. 'I'm sorry. Thank you, but I'm sorry.' She was hot and flushed and mortified and she still didn't know where to look. 'That was – unorthodox.'

He smiled. 'Hardly.'

She blinked. She gestured to her suit. 'You have a thing about rubber then?'

'Not,' calmly he unzipped her and began helping her ease the material away from her swimsuit and her sweat-damp bare limbs, 'until now.'

Kelly felt her colour deepen again and she wriggled to try and help him undress her. 'I'm sorry. Now's obviously not the best time to return the favour,' she mumbled.

'I'll survive.' He sounded laconic and she knew she'd amused him again. Avoiding his eyes, not yet quite herself, she concentrated on getting the suit off at her ankles. No way in the world could she have undressed completely to naked then so she pulled her shorts and top on directly over her togs.

When she was covered she straightened slowly then looked up and saw him watching her. She stiffened. 'Oh, my God.' Her gaze jerked to the door then back to Jack. 'I can't believe I let myself – I can't go out there. I can't just walk out like nothing happened. They'll all know.'

'How?'

One look at her face, she imagined, would probably do it. 'Haven't we been in her ages?' She'd left her watch on the side of the shower at the flat but she'd guess it had been half an hour. 'There's probably a queue to use it.'

'We've been five minutes.'

Five minutes! She stared at him. He'd done that – or more, he'd reduced her to that – in five minutes?

Jack, irritatingly cool-as-a-Popsicle, collected the suit she'd just worn along with the one she hadn't tried and opened the door, leaving her no choice but to clutch her bag to her chest and trail out. Despite his assurances she had expected to have half of Wellington queuing up waiting for them directly outside but in fact the shop was empty and the assistant was busy changing the paper roll at her till. She looked up when they came out and gave Kelly a brief, double take, but her eyes went immediately, dreamily, to Jack and then never left him.

He told her not to bother with a bag for the suit, that he'd carry it as it was and the transaction was over in a few seconds. Kelly was still too numb to think properly and it wasn't till they were back at Roger's car that she realised she'd let him pay for the suit, and even then she didn't feel up to arguing with him about it so she vowed to work it out later. 'So, are we going to your place to have sex properly now?' she asked when he signalled and turned the vehicle around.

The look that earned her was dry. 'You're not satisfied?'

She felt herself heating again. 'Hardly.' She deliberately echoed the word he'd used earlier. 'I'm appreciative, of course, but it was a solo effort. I want a whole lot more than that.'

'I can see you're going to be an extraordinarily demanding woman.' The look he sent her when they stopped for a crossing crowded with shoppers going in every direction was amused, but gently chiding. 'I've made plans for today. We're going to the beach.'

'And what about after the beach?'

'After the beach?' He moved his hand to her leg and slid it up under her shorts and she caught her breath but then the lights changed and he took his hand back, changed gear and accelerated away. 'If you're very good,' he darted her a quick, smiling look this time, 'then maybe, just maybe, I'll buy you lunch.'

Kelly called him a very rude name but he just laughed and so she folded her arms and stared out of the window and refused to talk to him. She meant to sulk but instead she found herself unable to stop her thoughts from replaying every second of those extraordinary minutes in the dressing room in excruciating, mortifying detail. Even more extraordinarily – she shifted uncomfortably in her seat and wound down her window in the hope that the breeze might cool her face – she felt herself becoming aroused again just from remembering.

Nymphomaniac, she accused herself silently. Harlot.

The boards on top of the car weren't surfboards, she discovered eventually, when she'd finally recovered her composure enough to be in a fit state to discover anything. They were the board parts of windsurfers, which is why there were straps on them to put your feet in. He took her to Seatoun, a long, shallow beach near the airport, and told her about the tide and the wind. And he told her that no matter how bad her sailing or how far she went off course, he'd always be close enough to rescue her before she could get far enough away from the beach to be in any danger.

With that reassurance behind her, she grew more interested. She'd often seen the boards zipping back and forth around the harbour and she'd admired the skills of their riders but never dreamed that she'd ever join them. But, she discovered, the more Jack explained, the more she was interested in learning. There was wind but almost no waves and as long as Jack stayed close she decided it was safe enough to risk trying it out.

She still had her togs on under her clothes and, blushing again at his gently knowing look, she put on the wet suit he'd bought for her, turning her back while Jack changed into his. His board was shorter than the one he'd brought for her, she saw. He unfurled the sails and connected them to the board, then showed her on land how to fit her feet into the grips on the board. He showed her how to haul up the sail and where to hold it for maximum control. So early in the day the beach and the wharf were deserted, apart from a man walking a happy-looking, rotund corgi along the sand. They left Jack's board on the beach, its sail sprawled to the side, and carried hers down to the water.

'I like this bit best,' Kelly told him when he threaded a harness between her thighs while she stood up to her knees in the sea. 'Mmm. Higher.' Her legs went weak again. She was still swollen from the time in the shop but she felt her flesh contract immediately in response to his inadvertent, teasing caress. 'Let's abandon the beach idea and go back to my place and just do this bit all day.'

'Greedy.' He withdrew his hand and slapped her tightly-covered bum. 'You're not getting out of this that easily.'

'Am I sexy?'

'Sweetheart, you are the sexiest woman I've ever met.'

'Then tell me, were you actually turned on earlier?' She looked at him very directly. 'Or if that was just a strange-shaped wallet I was feeling, would you mind if I borrowed it for a night, please?'

He laughed. 'Settle, Kelly.' He came closer, grabbing the board when it floated away from her. 'I had planned to string you out a little longer, I admit, but after today you have a better chance of being swallowed by a whale than you have of not feeling me inside you tonight. But now's not the time. So be a good girl and grab the sail.'

'Oh, my God.' Kelly cast an urgent, searching look around the shallow water surrounding them. 'There are whales here?'

It took over an hour for her to learn to stand up for more than a few seconds. He was patient and by the end of two hours her arms were aching so much they felt as if they might fall out of their sockets, but she could go quite a way along the beach and usually manage to stay on when she turned.

Jack, once he saw she had more confidence, headed out to where the sea was rougher. She admired the way he managed the craft but was content herself to drift up and back from the wharf, parallel with the beach.

Eventually she was too sore to do any more. He came in and they lazed on the sand while the sails dried then they packed away the equipment and drove further around the coast through the military base. They ate lunch in a café at Breaker Bay. 'I've finally figured out what your problem is.' Jack propped his legs up against the rail on the café's balcony, rocked his chair on to its two back legs and grinned at her.

'My problem is worrying that you're going to break your neck like that,' Kelly told him. 'Didn't your mother ever tell you to keep all four legs of your chair on the floor?'

His sunglasses concealed his eyes but she could feel them laughing at her, but he did, to her relief, let his chair drop back on to the flat. 'You're so used to saying you've no sense of adventure that you've started to believe it. Look at you today in the water. You had a great time.'

'Only because I knew there was no danger.' She straightened up suddenly when he grinned again. 'What? Did you lie about that?'

He lifted one broad shoulder. 'Maybe there was a small chance you might have been blown off course. The problem with Seatoun of course is that if you had, you'd have been right out of the harbour in five minutes and half-way to the South Island. Then there're the ferries of course. Unless you're looking out for them they'll take you by surprise. Most of them come in fast enough to take out even expert sailors – '

'You rat-bag!' She slapped the side of his arm with the back of her hand. 'You mean aside from being swallowed by a whale I could have drowned or been run over? How could you do that to me?'

'Calm down, calm down. I was watching.' He grabbed her fingers and squeezed them. 'You were safe enough. I'm just saying that you need to learn to spread your wings a little. Conquer your fear. Who knows, your whole life might change. You're not timid, Kelly. You might think you are, but you're not. Look at the play you made for me the day after we met. No timid woman would have pulled a stunt like that.'

'Perhaps desperation overcame my good sense,' she countered. 'And I never claimed to be timid. I'm not. I'm simply... fully aware of my own limits.'

'Well, you see, that's where you're wrong.' He released her fingers when she tugged at them, and reached out and stroked her hair where it had come loose from its knot. 'Because I don't think you've even begun to realise them.'

Kelly felt her heart thud. 'Going to expand my horizons, are you?' She meant to sound off-hand, careless, but the words came out dry and husky instead.

He didn't respond straight away. She held her breath, waiting. She tried to read his expression but the sunglasses were too much of a barrier.

Eventually he said quietly, 'If you let me.'

She looked away, stared out to sea. 'I don't think so, Jack. I'm happy with my horizons. It's only my sex life that I have a problem with.'

He didn't make any response, and when she looked back at him a few minutes later he was signalling for the bill and the time for lingering had obviously passed.

He took the direct way back to town around the airport. A quick check of her watch told her it was only two when he parked outside her flat. She felt grubby and sandy, she was in desperate need of a shower and her hair needed washing, but she could take care of all that in fifteen minutes, she calculated. He could have a cold drink while he waited. Geraldine always had beer in the fridge. Her paperwork and the chores and gardening she'd planned would wait another day.

Jack came around and opened her door then carried her bag and her wet suit up to the flat. She felt her colour darkening slightly as she opened the door but he barely looked at her. He carried everything in and dumped her wet suit into the bath, but then headed back to the front door without saying anything.

'Jack?' Kelly, getting a fright, raced after him. 'You're staying, aren't you?'

'Not now.' He didn't act as if there was anything the least bit strange about that. 'Don't forget what I told you about rinsing out the suit. It'll dry out side overnight.'

'Stop!' The word came out involuntarily but when he stilled by the gate she took a few steps outside. 'What about the whale? Remember? You said, less chance of...'

'Come and visit me later. I know somewhere we can go. Make it early, before five. OK?'

'Of course.' Did he think she was going to turn him down? 'I'll be there.'

Nervous but wanting to look nice, she left her hair loose the way he'd said he liked it and she wore her only good jewellery, gold earrings her father had given her for her twenty-first birthday, and her best dress. The ankle-length, summery, button-front red linen dress was more than five years old, but she'd hardly worn it and it still looked good, she thought.

Jack's approving look and smile when he opened his door to her at Karori was reward for her efforts. 'You look lovely.'

'This old thing,' she answered, deliberately off-hand, but his warm, knowing look told her he'd seen through her. He'd dressed up too, she saw. She hadn't seen the blue, immaculately pressed shirt or the dark slacks before and he looked strong and athletic and devastatingly attractive. Kiss me, she thought desperately. Kiss me.

But he didn't and she was left feeling lost. She might have found the courage to launch herself at him, forcing the issue, if his expression had been even remotely encouraging, but he seemed suddenly brisk and business-like and he was acting as if he was in a hurry to get her out of there.

She'd assumed that if they were going anywhere it'd be to a restaurant, but when he directed her to the Porsche and she climbed in, he apologised and passed her the three solid parcels he'd carried from the house.

She saw they were all thickly wrapped in layers of grease-proof-paper and plastic. 'The bigger two will fit here on top of the rest of this stuff,' he said, taking them from her again and placing them instead behind their seats, where, she saw, he'd already stacked another two boxes. 'The front's full already. Is this small one going to be too heavy to hold?'

'It's fine,' she assured him. But she was curious. 'It's a BYO cake?' she guessed doubtfully, fastening her seatbelt beneath the parcel. For a second she wondered if it could be meant for her, but then she remembered there was no way he could have found out. Bring your own restaurants were popular in Wellington, but the term generally implied alcohol. 'I smell chocolate.'

'Yep.' He'd come around beside her into the driver's seat and now he signalled and drew out on to the road. 'Dad has a major chocolate weakness. Tonight's my parents' fortieth anniversary. Tessa made the cakes for them. She's going to assemble them at the house and cream and ice them there. You don't mind, do you?'

She stared at him. 'What, do I mind that the cakes are chocolate?' she asked silkily. 'Do I mind holding this one? Or do I mind that you're dragging me all the way to Palmerston North and that I'll be intruding on a special family occasion?'

He signalled a turn out of the hospital grounds on to the road. 'About the chocolate of course.'

'I happen to love chocolate,' she informed him. 'Especially chocolate cake. And I'm happy nursing this but I'm not so sure I love where we're going. Jack. No doubt your parents are very nice, but what on earth are they going to think about you bringing me to such an important event?'

'Mmm, you're right,' he agreed. 'That might be a problem. They love me so much they won't believe you only want me for my body. Since it's such a big family occasion they'll assume the only reason you're there is that we're madly in love, contemplating having children together and about to announce our engagement.'

Kelly took a quick, sharp intake of breath but he just lifted one shoulder carelessly.

'If we don't do it tonight they'll say we're delaying it out of consideration for Mum and Dad's special day. Everyone will want to know your prospects and about the wedding plans, and about whether you've chosen a dress yet and how many bridesmaids you'll want, and watch out for Zoe because she'll try and muscle in on the wedding, she always does when there's one in the family. But you'll handle it, Kelly, I'm sure.'

'I know who I'll be wanting to handle. Not like that!' she said more violently, when he sent her a coolly reprimanding look. 'It might be better if you take me back now.'

'Too late.' They were at the start of the motorway now. 'It's a long drive and we're already overdue.'

Kelly knew Zoe because she was a junior doctor at Wellington hospital, and she knew Jack's brother, Nathan, too, of course, because he worked at Karori. But she was apprehensive after Jack's comments about meeting his family in such personal circumstances, yet in the event his smiling parents seemed, like everyone else, sanguine about her arrival with their eldest son. Only Nathan and Tessa, his wife, also a doctor from Karori, looked the slightest bit taken aback and even their assessment was pensive, she thought, rather than surprised, when they saw her arriving with Jack.

The party had been a surprise, she discovered, although Jack's parents had caught on when a hundred and fifty friends and relatives had begun arriving late in the afternoon with vague explanations about calling in for no particular reason. There was a DJ and music and plenty of food and drink and laughter and balloons, with celebrations in full swing by eight.

'I was worried,' Kelly told Zoe as they perused the huge buffet laid out on trestle tables under a marquee on the lawns outside the house, 'about what your parents would think.' At the younger doctor's blank look, she went on, 'About me being here with Jack. We're not going out, you see. Not seriously. I'm here more as a friend.'

But Zoe burst out laughing. 'Oh, I love that.' Inexplicably dressed, or at least inexplicably to Kelly, in a pink ballet tutu, tramping boots, a feather hat and a black leather jacket, Jack's sister flapped a pickled onion on a toothpick at her then drained a glass of punch. 'Tell Jack, he'll laugh too. And don't worry,' she went on expansively, swallowing her onion and thumping her glass down on to the table between a cheesecake and a kiwi-covered pavlova. 'Jack's with a different girl every time we see him. We all just assumed that you're his latest squeeze – ' Zoe broke off suddenly and clapped her toothpick hand over her mouth. 'Oops. Sorry, Dr West. I didn't mean that the way it came out.'

'It's Kelly,' Kelly said dryly. 'And that's OK.' She moved back to the main-course area of the table and helped herself to a slice of roast lamb. Jack had teased her deliberately, she realised now. He probably thought it hilarious that she'd been worried.

Later, after dinner and speeches, he steered her away from a conversation with two of his aunts, to dance. She told him what Zoe had said. They joined the other couples on the makeshift dance area in the gardens where guests had been shuffling and gyrating to ancient hits from the nineteen sixties and seventies. 'If you even hinted you were thinking about getting engaged, half of them would have heart attacks from the shock. Your Auntie Barbara's already apologised twice for forgetting my name but she says if she tried to remember the names of all her favourite nephew's girlfriends, her brain wouldn't have enough room left to remember her own address.'

'You know she's exaggerating.' Taking advantage of a near crash and a slowing of the pace of the music, Jack bent his head and bit her right earlobe in a gentle punishment that made her shiver. 'You're enjoying yourself then?'

'I am.' She tried to lift her arms to his shoulders but her upper arms and shoulders hurt so much from the morning's exercise she had to be content with resting them on his arms instead. 'I'm having a terrific time.'

It was true. Her own family was small and insular compared with his, and the vast web of relationships within and around his fascinated her. 'It's idyllic here. You must have had fun growing up.' The farm was small, she'd been informed, by New Zealand standards, but Jack's father had told her they ran around 1000 breeding ewes and 150 head of cattle, which sounded like a lot to her. 'I'm surprised any of you wanted to leave. It's strange all three of you children chose medicine instead of farming.'

'Our grandfather was the local GP for thirty years until he died.' The DJ announced he was taking a break, and Jack took her hand and they walked off away from the lights towards a group of sheds. Now the music had stopped, Kelly could hear sheep baa-ing all around them. She wondered if the party was keeping the poor creatures awake. 'In our school holidays we used to go with him on his rounds,' Jack continued. 'We thought we were helping.' He grinned. 'More likely we were getting in his way. But he was patient with us.'

She looked up at him. It was a clear, balmy night. The moon was only a little less than full in the sky and there was enough light to see fairly clearly. She opened a button on his shirt and slid a hand inside, seeking automatically and finding the hardened nubs of his nipples. 'You wouldn't have been in his way. He would have loved having you with him.'

'You think?' He drew her further into the shadows and opened her dress. She heard his swift, indrawn breath when he discovered her bare breasts. 'You're like this for me?'

'Yes.' He probed her and she tipped back her head, feeling her hair touch her waist as she arched in desire.

Jack of Hearts 157

'Do you like it?'

'Do you have to ask?' His voice was thick. He released her breast and held her waist, his fingers faster now, more urgent as he unfastened her dress completely. She was nude beneath, deliberately naked above the wide dark bands of her stockings at her thighs and she felt her body flushing and swelling with desire at his groan of discovery.

He lifted her into his arms and briefly she grabbed for sanity. 'Jack, we can't,' she protested faintly, when he carried her, one hand around her back, the other beneath her knees, past the barn and around the back of the party towards the dark side of the house. 'Not now. They'll miss us.'

He stopped but only to press his mouth to hers in an urgent caress. 'Do you think I care about that right now?'

chapter eleven

Kelly realised she didn't care either. At that moment, high in his arms, her mouth against his chest, she wouldn't have cared if the whole world knew.

He took her in through the rear entrance to the house, far away from the party, and upstairs and then up another flight in the dark. His movements were sure even without light and he was breathing fast, but he'd been like that even before he had lifted her, and the extra exertion of her weight seemed to make no difference to him. The room at the top, the only room in the loft of the house, looked like his mother's sewing room. There was a machine and patterns and fabric spread on the table, and an iron and board, but by the gable window, seductively alluring, illuminated by moonlight coming from above and from the side, was a day-bed.

Jack kick-slammed the door behind them and put her down on to the bed.

'My old bedroom,' he said gruffly, drawing back when she started to ask, his hand going to his shirt. 'There's nothing of me. Mum's not the sentimental type. But it's still mine in my head. And before you ask, no, no one else. Not since I was a kid.'

Beyond the distraction of her need and her excitement, Kelly was touched. She felt special that he'd brought her here, that she was the only one. She'd kicked off her heels when he'd put her on the bed and now she went to strip off the stockings, but seeing how his hands stilled and his eyes focused on the pale, gleaming thigh above the band, she changed her mind and left them on. Deliberately provocative, she parted her legs a little.

'Aren't you going to finish undressing?' she demanded huskily. His shirt was open but he was otherwise fully clothed.

'In a minute.' His gaze didn't shift. 'Keep going.'

Heat flooded her body. 'Like this?' she whispered, separating her legs another few centimetres. She'd never done anything like this before, she'd never deliberately exposed herself even a tiny amount to a man's gaze, but then until Jack she'd never felt this aroused before and the soft moonlight was pale enough to give her courage.

'More.'

She lay back on the pillows and covered her aching breasts with her hands. She lifted her knees. 'Like this?'

'More like this.' She heard him move, felt the depression of the bed when he knelt on it, then his hands took her hair and arranged it so that it cascaded beside her breasts and above her head and then he moved again and she felt his hands at her thighs. He spread her wide. 'Like this, Kelly. All the way.'

She gasped at the electric sensation of his mouth against her clitoris. The shock was so great that she shuddered and tried to close her legs, tried, urgently, to roll away but he grunted and held her fast and growled at her when she wriggled, and forced her still. When she finally gave in, defeated more by her own desire than by his strength and determination, he kissed her thigh and murmured approvingly and lowered his head again.

All knowing, expert fingers carefully opened her and when he touched her with his tongue, delicately, sensuously, she sank her teeth into her lower lip and shuddered silently, allowing him slowly, relentlessly, to explore every heated millimetre of the flesh he'd exposed.

She thought it would be fast. She thought she was so turned on that it might only take seconds again, but instead again and again her body stiffened and began preparing itself for pleasure only to be deprived when he stopped touching her at the last moment, teasing her and denying her relief and making her groan out loud and twist and dig her nails into his shoulders, and beg.

When at last the end came, when finally he let the delicate caress continue long enough for her to climax, the spasm was so strong and swift and powerful and it caught her so much by surprise that she wasn't prepared for it and she collapsed, her mind spinning, her body shaking uncontrollably, almost fainting with pleasure.

When she came around again, when the world eventually swam back into focus, she discovered him stretched out alongside her, stroking her hair.

Her limbs felt heavy and languid and drained but she reached out, began to lift herself to roll over him, wanting to complete the embrace they'd started, but Jack stopped her.

'Not here,' he murmured against her throat, gathering her against him. 'Not that. Later, hmm?'

'Mmm.' She could live with that, considering that she could barely lift her head. She collapsed on top of him, burying her face in the warm, wonderful scent of his chest through the opening of his shirt. His arms closed around her and she realised that she felt protected and enclosed and – paradoxically, considering how profoundly Jack disturbed her peace of mind – incredibly safe.

For a little while they lay quietly and her breathing slowly settled, then eventually she asked softly, continuing the discussion they'd started outside, 'Are your parents disappointed none of you want to take over the farm?'

He was still stroking her hair. He kissed it and surrounded his face with it, and then he moved his head and slid lower and she caught her breath when he licked her nipple. 'They want us to be happy,' he answered huskily against her skin. 'Neither Mum nor Dad is sentimental and they've always encouraged us to go out into the world and explore and do whatever we wanted.'

'That's so different from my family,' Kelly said, her voice catching as his tongue lightly caressed her.

'Your parents weren't happy about you going off to med school?'

'More mystified,' she admitted. He'd stilled and now he rolled her over on to the bed and propped himself on one elbow beside her, watching her, stroking her breasts.

'Both of them love books and reading but neither of them went to university and my sister left school when she was sixteen. But I didn't leave home to go to varsity, I lived with my parents until my wedding day. My sister and her family still live around the corner from Mum. Celia married the boy next door, literally. She's spent all her life within half a mile of where we were born. She jokes about it all the time.' Only sometimes Celia didn't sound as if she was joking. 'Celia would have liked to do more I think,' she went on slowly. 'She had her first baby when she was seventeen and she has four children now, and they don't have a lot of money.'

'She envies you?'

Kelly avoided answering that. 'She thinks getting pregnant so early stopped her going to university.' His hand spread over her breast, flattening it, and she covered it with her hand, encouraging the exploration. Her nipple tingled still from his mouth and she was surprised that he'd been able to arouse her again so quickly. 'She has this crazy idea my life is a riot. I've tried to persuade her to come and visit so that she'll understand what hours I work and how drab my social life is, how *non-existent* it is, most of the time, but she won't. She's like Dad that way, only not pathologically so, thank goodness. He was severely agoraphobic.'

Jack's expression turned concerned and she shrugged weakly. 'He had an accident at work when we were quite young and he was badly injured. His back was permanently damaged and he was never able to work again. After he came home from hospital he gradually grew more afraid of leaving the house. He could manage the nearby streets, if he worked at it he could walk around the block, but going any further panicked him. He'd always been a homebody, we all were really, so none of us thought that was strange. I was so blind, because although eventually I studied psychiatry at med school, I still never applied that teaching to my own father. It was only after he died and I listened to his friends giving the eulogy at the funeral that I finally realised he hadn't been shy, he'd been ill. I've always wondered since whether if I'd only realised sooner, I might have been able to make a difference to his life.'

He gathered her against him again and held her, murmuring comfort, and she blinked fast to ward off the tears – the grief was always there in the background but the years had dulled it enough to make it bearable most of the time – and pressed her face into his warm chest.

'Celia doesn't see that I'm playing with the cards I've been dealt the best way I can, the same way she is,' she continued in a muffled voice after a little while, when she had her emotions collected again. 'If I told her I'd swap with her in an instant, she wouldn't believe me.'

'Would you?'

She thought of her niece and nephews. 'Sometimes.'

'I've suddenly developed an intense dislike for your brother-in-law.'

His voice rumbled against her face and Kelly felt her introspection dissolve. She laughed and lifted herself away to kiss him. 'I meant, because of the children, not the husband. But I do like William. He's kind and gentle, and he has infinite patience with Celia, even if that might not always be the best way to manage my sister. However, my feelings for him are strictly platonic.'

He kissed her nose and hugged her and then played with her hair again, arranging it so that it framed her breasts before he stroked them again.

The feeling of being cherished and sheltered was suddenly far more unsettling than being merely aroused by him would have been. Kelly stiffened and moved away slightly and propped herself up on her elbows.

Jack let her go. He observed her movements with shadowed eyes but he didn't comment.

Talking mainly to overcome the unease his embrace had just engendered she crossed her arms under her head, rested back and went on, 'Even with Dad not being well, I had a very happy upbringing. I know it must seem strange to you,' she gestured around at the room and towards the windows and the vast rural landscape that she knew stretched beyond them, 'because you grew up amidst this beauty and space, but we found joy in our little house. I didn't feel we were missing anything.'

'Are you supporting your mother and your sister? Is

that where the money goes?'

'I wish it was.' Her mother still had money from her father's accident compensation settlement, but William and Celia could have done with something extra. Judging from Celia's acid comments over the past five years, her sister had noticed she was spending less on the children's birthday and Christmas gifts than she once had, but by next year she hoped to be able to be more generous.

Her eyes picked out the slow, blinking progress of a satellite amidst the star-sprinkled sky above them. She could hear, beyond the house, the music starting up again.

She turned her head and looked at Jack, studied him for a few moments, then said, 'When I was married to Warwick I put my signature to some loans he wanted to take out.' It felt dangerously intimate, this telling, because it was in her nature to keep her problems to herself, but she'd told him so much now. And it wasn't so bad. What could be more intimate than what they'd just done? He knew about the miscarriages and about her father and Celia and about how she envied her sister her children. He knew almost everything. Withholding the rest seemed suddenly not such an important thing.

'He speculated on currency movements. I knew there was a theoretical risk we could lose our savings and the cars and even the house, but something went wrong and it ended up far worse than that. The banks took everything but we were still left with huge debts. Warwick skipped overseas and so they came after me for the rest of the money. When the whole nightmare began I made a vow to myself that I'd work like crazy for five years so that I could be free of debt by the end of it. That way I get my life back again, instead of having the mistakes I've made weighing on my shoulders for ever. As long as nothing disastrous goes wrong and I keep up the repayments, I should have all the money paid off on schedule by the end of this year.'

'How much was the initial loan?'

She told him the figure and saw him start. 'How could they come after you?' he demanded. 'You can't have known what you were signing... '

'I did. When we arranged everything in the beginning, they insisted I took independent advice. I signed anyway. And later when it all fell apart, I knew that as long as the banks were reasonable about how long they could give me, which they were once they realised I wasn't going to default on the loans, there was never any question I'd eventually be able to pay everything back. And I have. Almost.'

There was as much space as there could have been between them given the narrowness of the bed but now he reached out and touched her shoulder. 'Why sign for the loans when you had advice not to?'

'He was my husband.'

'That's a fact, not a reason.' He sounded impatient. He sat up and swung round, lifting one leg over the other, his eyes very dark in the shadowed light. 'He had no right to jeopardise your security. Didn't your parents try to persuade you to say no?'

'I didn't tell them about it. The numbers we were talking would have horrified them. They'd have worried too much. By the time it all went wrong, Dad was ill and it wouldn't have been fair to burden them with it then. They were upset when we separated but Celia had dropped hints to them about what Warwick was like and they thought I initiated the divorce. Dad died a few months after it came through.'

'If – Warwick has the money now, you could sue him for it, couldn't you? To recover the debts or at least his half of the amount? Have you spoken to a solicitor? He or she would need to see your divorce settlement, but a civil suit might still be possible.'

'I've spoken to several lawyers over the years. Not one has rated my chances of getting anything out of him much above nil. Warwick's not stupid and money was always very important to him. He was furious when the banks took the house. He'll have made sure that any assets he has this time are too tied up for anyone to touch.'

'It still has to be worth a try, doesn't it? Do you know where he is?'

'Not exactly, although I know how to find out.' She hadn't heard from her ex-husband directly since the day he flew out of New Zealand, but his mother's annual Christmas card always mentioned him. 'It would cost a lot to chase him.'

'I'll pay.'

She ignored that. She swung round and sat on the end of the bed, looking for her dress. 'Next year, when I have enough money of my own again to be able to think about it, I'll see another lawyer.'

'How could you love a man who'd do that to you?'

She forgot the dress. Her lashes fluttered down. 'You don't always choose whom you love. If you're young and silly, or if you don't have your wits about you, it just happens. Warwick was very attractive. Unfortunately I wasn't the only woman to think so.'

He stared at her. 'He must have been mad.'

She smiled brief appreciation for that. 'He loved women.' The same way Jack did. 'He loved me in his own way. He had affairs, but he always came back.'

It had taken her a long time to realise what was going on. In the early years of her marriage she'd been too busy trying to balance the demands of her career with being a good wife and trying to have the baby they both wanted to notice anything. But one weekend she'd come home unexpectedly when she was supposed to be working.

The shock of finding another woman in their bed had been profound. At first she'd blamed herself. She'd assumed he had to be looking for something she lacked, or that the miscarriages and her failure to produce a son for him had put him off her as a woman.

But his fevered apologies and declarations of love and need, and his obvious desire for her and his continued lovemaking had been at odds with that. Eventually, when there were more women, she'd been forced to accept that men like her husband never changed.

'I thought I could make it work. Our relationship was still strong. Even when he had another woman, he never stopped sleeping with me.' She watched him carefully, knowing from his sharp intake of breath that she'd shocked him finally. 'He'd have his girlfriends but they never lasted long and I loved him so I always took him back. The night he told me about the money, he asked me to go to Europe with him. He wanted us to run away from all our debts and never come back. That was the night I fell out of love with him. It was probably the best thing that could have happened to me. Sometimes I think that if it hadn't been for the loans, we'd still be together and nothing would ever have changed.'

'You'd have seen sense eventually. You're an intelligent woman.'

'I don't know. I don't know if I could have walked away from him. In those days I thought marriage vows were sacred. If it hadn't been for the money, I think I'd have stayed with him for ever.' She lowered her eyes again. 'So now you know. It's not pretty, I know, but you must see now that I'm not some delicate, innocent flower who knows nothing about the world and who needs to be cosseted and reassured. You don't have to pretend you have any special feelings or plans for me, Jack. The reason I'll never want anything but sex from you is because I will never let a man like you tie me in knots the way Warwick did.'

chapter twelve

Jack studied the soft, vulnerable curve of Kelly's neck. He understood now, finally, why she was so defensive with him, and he wanted to take her in his arms and never let her go. 'I'm not your ex-husband, Kelly. I am nothing like him. I have not behaved well all my life, but I would never treat you or any other woman that way. It's safe for you to trust me.'

'No it isn't.' She sounded careless as if it didn't matter particularly. 'I'm in danger every minute I'm with you. Because you are like him. You're just the same. You like women, the same way he did, you flirt and play around just like he did, you even sound like him sometimes when you're trying to persuade me to do something you know I don't want to do. He used to know the same tricks you do. He used to try and use sex the same way you do, to get me to do what he wanted. It's funny. I used to think I'd be immune to that now but you're even better at getting your own way like that than he was. I used to think he had to have spoiled me for all other men, but meeting you has taught me he hasn't. Meeting you has made everything worse for me because now I understand how vulnerable I still am.

'I don't think about phantom lovers any more, instead I lie awake at night imagining *you* there with me. I want to touch you and feel you against me. I want to feel your weight on me. I'm becoming obsessed. I can't stop imagining how it will feel when you push inside… '

'That's enough,' he interjected, but she held up her hand, her small face shadowed but determined.

'By saying you're like Warwick, I don't mean you look similar, but he was dark too, a bit more thickset, but about the same height as you. He was strong too, like you. Physically at least.'

Mute with shock, he saw she almost smiled at that. 'If I hold my eyes half closed,' she whispered, 'I could almost pretend you are him.'

He felt like strangling her then, but instead he simply stood up from the bed. 'I'll get your dress. We must have left it outside.'

The sound of his blood pumping was like a raging surf in his ears. It took him only a few minutes to retrieve the dress from by the barn and return it to her. He stood silent, savagely silent, while she dressed, and then he reached out. Taking extreme care to keep his grip controlled, he put his hand in the small of her back and turned her towards the stairs then out of the house towards the party.

'It's late,' he observed, as urbanely as he could manage. The disco was still playing and he'd paid the DJ to stay until one but the ceremonial part of the evening was over and his parents wouldn't miss them if they left now. 'Say your farewells then I'll drive you home to collect your car. Not a word,' he commanded abruptly, when she sent him a pale look and seemed about to speak. 'If you know what's good for you, Kelly, you won't say another bloody word.'

He put loud music on in the car. He felt her gaze on his face from time to time on the way back to Wellington but his concentration on the road was near to total and he took no notice. It occurred to him, as he changed down for a sharp corner ahead, that he must be scaring her, but he didn't care. Neither of them spoke until he drew up outside his townhouse.

He meant her to go straight to her car, and he saw her stiffening when she realised that. 'I need to come in to use the bathroom,' she said challengingly, looking up at him when she stepped out on to the footpath.

He wanted her to leave immediately yet her words left him no choice but to let her into the house. He waited for her to go ahead of him then walked into the kitchen and opened a beer from his fridge. The liquid was cold against the dryness of his throat and he drained it in a few long swallows, before helping himself to a second.

Halfway through it, he heard a sound. He lowered the bottle and surveyed Kelly. Instead of leaving of her own accord as he'd expected, she'd come to the doorway. He studied her as neutrally as he could bring himself to, considering the violence of his emotions. 'Yes?' He watched dispassionately as slow colour crept across her throat. 'Did you want something?'

The colour lifted to her face. 'Nothing beyond the obvious. This morning at the beach you intimated that we would be having sex tonight. When you carried me to your room this evening I didn't get the impression that you'd changed your mind. I realise you're annoyed about the things I told you about Warwick, but I was wondering if making love was still a possibility... '

'At this precise moment I would rather cut off my right leg. If that changes, I'll let you know.'

The colour took over her entire face. 'Fine,' she said crisply. 'Fine.' She folded her arms across her chest, but didn't move. 'Do you have my mobile number?'

'If I need it, I can get it.' He put his half-empty bottle down on to the bench with a hard thump and eyed her wearily when she still didn't make any attempt to leave. 'I won't need it,' he growled.

'You should be relieved,' she burst out. 'Can't you forget your monumental ego for once and just be relieved that all I'll ever want from you is sex?'

He was frustrated and aggrieved and coldly furious, but he wasn't relieved. He retrieved his beer and lifted it to his mouth, and when she was still there when he finished it, he sent the bottle crashing into the recycling bin. When she still didn't move, he went through the arch connecting the kitchen with his living area and from there the stairs and his bedroom. 'Shut the door on your way out.'

He meant not to listen. He meant not to feel. He meant to climb calmly into bed after his shower and not care where she was or what she was doing or how she was feeling, but after ten minutes in bed he knew he wasn't going to be able to sleep knowing she was there. He rolled out of bed and folded the towel he'd discarded after his shower, around his hips. He checked at the window in case his instincts had misled him and he'd missed her leaving, but her car hadn't moved. He opened his door and went downstairs.

Kelly was in his living room. She'd turned on a lamp in the corner and kicked off her shoes, and she stood in her stockinged feet looking out of his window on to the street. She must have heard his feet on the stairs because she spoke as soon as he came into the room. 'I don't want to leave, Jack. Not after today. Not after everything that's happened. If you force me to go, you'll be humiliating me.' She turned around. 'Is that what you're trying to do?'

He felt his jaw tighten. '"Humiliating you",' he echoed in a hollow voice. He wondered if she even understood the concept. 'Tell me, how – '

'I made a complete fool of myself practically dissolving in front of you not just once but twice today. Of course it's humiliating that you can just walk away after that. I didn't want it to be just me. I didn't want you to do me a favour! I thought that we were both involved. I wanted us to both be involved. And besides,' she looked at the window again, 'it's my birthday. And I'm sorry, I realise this must sound pathetic, but I don't want to spend another birthday night on my own.'

'It's your birthday?' That shook him. '*What*? Why didn't you tell me?'

'Because it doesn't matter. I don't care about it. If you have to do something, then let me stay.'

He sighed. He didn't want to go near her but still he walked over to her and lifted her into his arms for the second time that night. 'I won't touch you,' he warned, carrying her towards the stairs. But it was a hollow vow, and he knew from the way she opened her mouth against his throat as he carried her up that she knew it too, and that even his anger wouldn't protect him.

He put her down on the bed then came after her, intent at first just on holding her calmly and steadily and without emotion, determined to soothe her hurt feelings then send her away. But she was soft and warm and breathless and willing, and her whispered pleas and her hands on his skin and the silk and scent of her hair and skin worked under his defences and into his senses, and against his will he found his hands stroking and seeking and loosening her hair then sliding away her dress to bare her breasts and her thighs.

When she twisted away from him, when she unbalanced him and turned the aggressor, when her mouth and her hands, urgent now, surrounded his sex, he knew, even though that wasn't what he wanted from her now, that he was lost. He was strong but not strong enough to resist her when she was like this. She'd beaten him and he surrendered willingly. She came over him, spreading her legs, and he slid his hands under her and balanced her and kissed her breasts, and she kissed his chest and touched his face and called out his name, and there was nothing in the world he could have done then to stop himself surging into the tight, incredible welcoming warmth of her embrace.

Kelly fell asleep within minutes of her final climax. He lay awake the few remaining hours until dawn, then carefully he turned her on to her side away from him. He pulled on swimming shorts and joggers, grabbed a towel and his keys and headed out.

He was gone at least three hours. He'd left his watch on the floor by the bed but the chill and softness had gone from the air by the time he was parking outside the townhouse.

His neighbour was out front collecting one of the Sunday newspapers that had been delivered to his lawn. 'Morning,' the other doctor called out, with a wave and a grin. 'You're keen. How's the water?'

'Cold.' Jack wiped the towel he wore round his neck over his forehead. The water at Makara had been icy and he'd been freezing when he first climbed out of the water, but after he'd run himself deliberately hard down the coast and back over the hills to the car park he'd needed another swim to cool himself down. 'The surf should be good today up on the coast.' He remembered the surgeon had mentioned that he had custody of his two children for the weekend. 'It's forecast to warm up later. It'll be a good day to choose if the kids want to hit the waves.'

'Good idea,' his neighbour answered. 'We might borrow a couple of your boards again if you're not using them.'

'If I'm not around, grab them from the back.' Jack lifted his hand in acknowledgement, collected his own paper, wiped his face and his chest again and put his key in the lock.

He'd expected Kelly to be gone by the time he got back, but her car was still outside. He found her curled in his bed in the same position she'd been in when he left her, still fast asleep, her glorious hair spread across the pillows and down her back.

He studied her broodingly for a few seconds then forced himself to walk away. His movements brisk and efficient, he dumped his shorts and the wet towel into the laundry hamper in his bathroom, grabbed a fresh one and headed for the shower.

Kelly slept through the sound of the water and him dressing, and he left her there. He closed the door and went downstairs to make coffee and stared at his paper for most of the rest of the morning. Finally, after hours, he heard movement above him then steps and then, eventually, she came looking for him.

'Sorry. You should have woken me.' She'd put her dress and her shoes back on but she'd left her legs bare, and her loose hair swung against her elbows as she moved. His fingers ached to reach for it, he longed to feel the silky slide of it between his hands again, but he stayed right where he was.

'I only have instant.' He nodded to the coffee. 'Want some?'

'Please.' The hesitant way her eyes tracked his movements while he prepared the drink told him she was nervous, but since she couldn't be any more tense about this than he was, he held back. 'What's this?' she asked, after a few seconds.

He turned around and saw her examining the shell he'd carried from the beach. 'It's for you. For your birthday yesterday.' He grimaced. 'I'm sorry, I should have thought to take money when I went out – '

'No, I like it,' she interrupted. 'A lot. It's beautiful. And you already bought me a present, the wet suit. Yesterday. Remember?' She turned the shell round a couple of times, then held it to her ear. 'I can hear the sea.'

He frowned. 'Kelly...'

'I thought last night was fun,' she interrupted again, quickly this time, as if she wanted to get in first. 'A lot of fun. Really. I was wondering if we could do it again some time?'

Fun. She'd had fun. He'd given her his soul and she'd had fun. His hand tightened compulsively on the spoon he was using to stir her drink. Keeping his expression controlled he said, 'Sure.' Over his dead body. 'I'll call you.' Like maybe when the sky fell in. He dropped the spoon into the sink. *'Some time.'*

'You'll call me,' she echoed. She put the shell down carefully. 'Ah.'

'Ah.' He put the coffee on the breakfast bar and slid it towards her. 'Toast?'

'I'm not hungry.' She sat slowly on one of the stools on the living room side of the bar, opposite him. 'And I don't understand. I was under the impression that you enjoyed yourself as much as I did.'

'So what do you want?' he demanded wearily. 'Balloons and whistles? Grow up, Kelly. You wanted to play it this way, so don't complain. Sex is sex. Sometimes it's mediocre, often it's good, frequently it's great, rarely it's extraordinary. The one thing it never does is change anything.'

Small flags of colour crept into her cheeks. 'I didn't expect it to,' she said, her tone defensive. 'I'm not interested in any sort of relationship, of course I'm not, I wasn't saying that. I'm not trying to change that. All I was asking was whether you might want to repeat the experience...'

'I gave you what you wanted.' Deliberately, he returned to his paper. 'As I said, I'll call you.'

'Well, I'm sorry it was all such a chore for you.' He heard the scrape as she pushed her untouched drink away. 'I'll be on my way then.' She walked over and grabbed her handbag from where she'd left it on the couch the night before, her movements, he saw, unnaturally stiff. 'Before I make an even bigger nuisance of myself by outstaying my welcome.' She grabbed her shell from the breakfast bar then took a fast step back, as if she expected him to try and snatch it away from her again. 'I'll check the wards before I go, make sure Roger's not having any problems with any of our children.'

'Leave it,' he ordered. 'Go home. I'll go over when I've finished the paper.' He generally called into the wards every day over the weekend. 'Most of the kids are mine at the moment anyway.'

Roger was in. He looked harassed but managed a grin when Jack came up to him once he'd finished checking the wards.

'Anything major?' Jack asked.

'The usual,' Roger told him. 'But plenty of it. My reg is transferring a six-year-old with pneumonia who needs ventilation into our last ICU bed and we're waiting for the chopper to take a newborn in heart failure up to Auckland.'

'Need an escort?'

He was happy to help out, but Roger explained that Margie Lomax was going with the baby. 'She's covering ICU for the weekend.'

'Hi, Jack.' Tania came up to them carrying mugs and chocolate biscuits. 'Afternoon tea for the doctors,' she announced. 'A special treat because it's Sunday and you're all working so hard. As long as you don't start expecting it,' she added, laughing when they both stared at her in astonishment. 'Hey, I don't only run the wards, you guys. I see my job as staff morale officer too. I know how to make a hot drink as well as anyone else round here.'

'Ah, I remember the days when all nurses made tea for doctors,' Roger said nostalgically. 'I even remember when they fed us toast – '

'You're pushing the boundaries, Roger.' Tania slapped his arm with the unopened packet of macaroons. 'Quit before you get yourself in trouble.'

Roger's bleep went off before he could say anything more, and he muttered something about that being Margie and went for the phone.

'How did yesterday go?' Jack asked Tania. He knew she'd agreed to let her estranged husband return home the day before.

'He's on his best behaviour,' she said, with a smile. 'So that's a start, at least. It's all right so far.' She nodded. 'He's changed. He seems to appreciate more what he gave up. I'm keeping my distance still, for now, but I think it might work this time.'

'I hope so,' Jack said sincerely. 'He was a fool to leave.'

'Thanks.' She squeezed his arm. 'By the way, Kelly was in just before you got here.'

Jack regarded her mildly. Clearly Kelly hadn't taken his advice to leave the wards for him. 'And?' he prompted when Tania kept looking at him.

She laughed. 'Don't *and* me, Jack McEwan. I'm not stupid. And I'm all for it, as long as you keep it fun for her. But she didn't look happy today, in fact I thought she seemed quite distraught. If you dare hurt that poor girl, then,' she beamed at him, 'my staff and I will gang up and break both your legs.'

'Break both my legs,' he echoed.

'Mmm. Which would be a shame,' she went on soulfully, her gaze dropping. 'Because they are such – beautiful legs. Such strong, hard, masculine, powerful…'

'Tania,' Jack chided. He put a finger under her chin and tilted her head up to him, meeting her dancing brown eyes solemnly. 'You would do that, to me, for Kelly?'

'We all would,' she confirmed cheerfully. 'But don't get me wrong, we know she deserves some excitement in her life. In fact I told her to go for you…'

'You told her *what*?'

'To go. For you.' She smiled. 'I told her you were definitely worth a try.'

Jack groaned. Women. You could never trust them. 'Tania…'

'It was girl talk, Jack. Don't fret. She knows I wasn't serious.'

'But now you're panicking because if she by any chance ends up taking your advice and gets hurt, you'll feel guilty.'

She flushed. 'Mmm. I will.'

'But does it work the other way?' he enquired gently.

'What if your precious Kelly has hurt me? Will you break her legs? What if I'm the one who's been left with a broken heart?'

But Tania grinned at him. 'As if.'

Jack moved his thumb across her chin. 'Tania?'

'Hmm?'

'Butt out.'

'OK.' She smiled. 'I'm going to try and trust you.'

He finished his coffee, put the mug down on her tray, and helped himself to a chocolate macaroon, 'I wouldn't,' he warned, taking a bite of the coconut-filled biscuit on his way out. 'I really wouldn't go *that* far!'

chapter thirteen

Kelly quickly realised she had no choice but to do her best to be sophisticated about having slept with Jack. He was right after all, he *had* given her exactly what she'd asked for. And that was all she'd wanted. And it was all she wanted now. She just wanted more of it.

But now, after the humiliation of him turning her down, the only face-saving thing she could do was to act as if she knew what it was all about and that everything was perfectly fine.

Even if it did feel as if nothing was ever going to be fine again.

She spent Monday in Wellington and he'd already left by the time she arrived out at Karori for her night on call. On Tuesday she behaved with absolute normality, she thought, on the round. As if nothing untoward had ever happened.

She arrived at the canteen for her lunch with Margie and Sarah and discovered that Tessa Webster – Jack's bubbly sister-in-law who was an obstetric registrar at the hospital and another member of the medical women's group – had joined them. She smiled and said how nice, and when Tessa went on to ask how she'd enjoyed the party on Saturday night, she didn't even flinch.

'It was great,' she answered enthusiastically. 'Your chocolate cake was out of this world.'

Tessa looked pleased. 'I'm good with desserts,' she confided. 'That one was made with almonds instead of flour so that's why it was so rich. We don't like giving Thomas too many sugary things and Nathan doesn't have a sweet tooth, so I hardly ever get to bake these days. I'm glad you liked it.'

Sarah listened interestedly through all of this. 'And this was...?' she prompted.

'Jack's parents' wedding anniversary,' Kelly explained. 'He didn't have a date to take so I went with him.'

'Jack didn't have a date to take,' Sarah echoed mildly. 'Jack. Hmm. Intriguing.'

'I had a wonderful time,' Kelly went on, avoiding Sarah's speculative look. 'There was music and dancing and lots of good company, and the food was fantastic.'

'Kelly...'

'It sounds lovely,' Margie interrupted, to Kelly's relief talking over whatever it was Sarah had been about to say. But Margie didn't stay around because her bleep shrilled. She put her hand over it dulling the noise, excused herself and headed for one of the canteen's internal phones.

'Oh, there's Jack now,' Tessa said suddenly, and Kelly looked round in fright, feeling her nerves, already jangling, go on red alert at the sight of her colleague in the sandwich queue. 'I promised Mr Solomon I'd warn him about a caesarean we're doing soon. He wants me to ask Jack to come. I'm right thinking Jack's the kids' consultant on call today, isn't he, Kelly?'

'As far as I know,' Kelly confirmed.

'Won't be a sec.' Tessa skipped away to see him, leaving Kelly and Sarah alone at the table.

Kelly dared a quick, sideways glance, but Sarah laughed. 'Don't fret, I'm not going to ask. Not that I wouldn't love to know, of course, but we both know Margie would decapitate me if I dared offend you.'

'You wouldn't offend me.' Kelly lowered her head. 'I just – well I think I might be a little out of my depth,' she admitted heavily. *A little*? That had to be in the running for the understatement of the year.

Sarah looked concerned. 'Are you all right?'

'Mmm.' Her braid had fallen across her chest and she pushed it back over her shoulder. 'I think. Sort of.' Even if you wanted to, how did you explain something like this? she wondered.

How did you explain that what you'd blithely expected to be a heated few hours of sexual passion had instead turned into hours of slow, absorbed, intensely loving mutual exploration building repeatedly to such sweetly tender crescendos that she'd been left as drained emotionally as she was physically, so exhausted in his arms and so deeply asleep that she'd not stirred for ten hours?

And how did you explain that something she'd assumed would make her feel refreshed and cheerful and renewed and back in control of her emotions, had instead devastated her senses and now left her confused and sad and panicked?

She'd thought she'd be able to walk away from him unscathed. But she'd been wrong.

Until Saturday – before the dive shop – she'd assumed she knew everything there was to know about sex and about her own responses. But nothing, *nothing*, with Warwick had even come close to matching her experience with Jack.

The things he did to her, the way he could make her feel and respond, the way he could drive her senseless with need, the way she wanted to touch him, the way she felt driven to make him feel the same way, was all new to her. It could have been shocking and base, it was *still* shocking, but what had elevated the experience above everything she'd dreamed was that, beyond the passion and urgency, his lovemaking had also been tender and loving and devastatingly moving.

He'd stroked her and caressed her and murmured things to her that had turned her wild, and other things that had soothed her shock and had calmed her when she needed to be calmed lest she go mad. He'd excited her when she wanted to be excited and he'd gentled her when she needed to be gentled. In her whole life she'd never felt as loved and as cherished as she'd felt in those precious hours with him before she'd fallen asleep in his arms.

She'd thought she knew all about love, too. Before. Now she realised she hadn't even begun to know about it.

She knew she'd insisted that she wanted their encounters to be casual, but that tenderness had changed everything. She was in love with him. She could never tell him, of course. It was hard enough admitting it to herself. Wanting, even in her head, even for one second, to spend the rest of her life with another womanising man was pretty much like wanting to jump into a vat of boiling oil every morning. Yet that didn't mean it wasn't just as painful to walk away.

So how, given that, could she possibly find words to explain the agony of Jack's casual brush-off on Sunday morning? How could she explain the confusing irony that what she knew was good for her, what she knew was the very best result for her, instead hurt like nothing had ever hurt her before.

And how did you explain how thinking about him with Tania or Donna Ling or Robert Bingham's PA made her want to cry?

And wouldn't Sarah think she was mad if she knew that

a small, unpolished shell had suddenly become her most precious possession in the world?

She smiled in an effort to reassure the other woman. 'So what did you do at the weekend?' she asked. 'Did you go up to the holiday house?' Sarah and Robert and the children regularly spent weekends at the Kapiti Coast, an hour or so north from Wellington. 'The weather would have been lovely for it.'

'Oh, it was terrific,' Sarah said obligingly, smiling back. 'Bobby took Louise and one of her friends fishing both days but the rest of us spent most of the time at the beach.'

Tessa came back. 'Jack's had to rush off but he says to remind you there's a rep coming to talk to both of you at a quarter-to,' she said to Kelly. 'Your secretary bleeped him to say she's on her way. You're supposed to meet on Maui ward somewhere.'

'In the seminar room,' Kelly said jerkily, nodding. Until then she'd forgotten about the session. She wouldn't be alone with Jack because the pharmaceutical company rep would be there, of course, and Spencer and some of the other junior doctors, but a quick glance at her watch warned her she only had ten minutes to go. She felt her stomach flutter. 'Thanks.'

Spencer and the juniors were already waiting with Jack when she arrived on the ward. She greeted the other doctors in a general way, met Jack's enigmatic look with contrived calm, left a gap between them and took the next seat along.

The rep rushed in late, full of apologies, and gave them sandwiches, juices, free pens and writing pads.

Kelly had already eaten, the juice was the cordial kind and full of sugar, and her pen didn't work. The pad was emblazoned with the name of the rep's pharmaceutical company, and far too big to be practical, the woman barely looked at her and Kelly wasn't impressed with the presentation. It didn't help that the anti-allergy drug the rep was trying to promote was twice as expensive as the one they normally used. Considering that the cheap alternative had a similar spectrum of activity and side-effect profile, the woman was wasting her time, because at that cost there was no way Kelly was ever going to advocate the antihistamine to the board who approved medications for the hospital's supply list.

Nor did it help that the woman was profoundly flirtatious and obviously, despite the longing looks her cleavage was earning from Spencer and the other juniors, extremely taken with Jack.

Kelly averted her eyes when the younger woman, laughing at a joke Spencer had made, one which hadn't even been funny, rocked forward on her chair, exposing yet more of her breasts, and put her hand on one of Jack's knees.

'You have such a great sense of humour, Dr McEwan,' she gushed, conveniently forgetting, Kelly noted dully, that it had been Spencer who'd made the comment.

Kelly stood up. 'I've a clinic to get to. Thank you, Ms Wilson. Spencer, are you coming?'

'Be there soon, Dr West.' The registrar's eyes were still focused somewhere around the middle of the rep's chest. Kelly grimaced and briefly brooded about the fickleness and foolishness of men, but at least with Spencer and the SHOs there the woman couldn't actually jump on Jack which was some tiny consolation, and so she left them to it.

Clinic was full. 'I've had to add six on the end,' the

nurse looking after the session explained. 'Sorry, Kelly, but they all sounded urgent. Is that OK?'

'Of course.' Kelly nodded. Carol had been covering Paediatric Outpatients at Wellington and now Karori for a total of twenty-five years. If she thought the referrals were urgent, they were urgent. 'Who's this?' she asked, lifting the top, thick set of notes. She didn't recognise the name.

'Oh, that one's for Jack,' Carol exclaimed. She clicked her tongue. 'A young girl who's had rheumatic fever. I'll take them through to him.'

Kelly passed her the files. They seemed to be getting more cases of rheumatic fever, she thought, making a mental note to look up the figures to check whether that were true. The illness, where the body overreacted to what was usually a short-lived throat infection, could lead to serious joint and heart valve damage.

'Jack might be a few minutes late,' she warned Carol. 'He and Spencer are still with a rep upstairs. She seemed to have her eye on Jack.'

'Don't we all?' Carol chuckled. 'I'll take this through. Your first child's in Two. He's a new referral with early morning coughing. Sounds like asthma, if you ask me.'

'Thanks.' *Don't we all*. Kelly reached for the notes. Wasn't that the truth.

Reluctant to keep the children and their parents waiting any longer than they had already, Kelly skipped afternoon tea. Jack, called away for the caesarean section Tessa had mentioned, had to leave early in the session and he put his head round the door to warn her and she nodded absently. But he was away longer than she expected and she saw a dozen of his patients, including the child Carol had told her about with rheumatic fever, to keep the waiting time down on his side of the list.

Tala's mother seemed anxious, and when Kelly probed she discovered that she was worried about more than Tala's illness. Her husband had recently lost his job when the factory he'd worked at for three years had been closed. Because he'd been employed as a contract worker, rather than a permanent employee, he hadn't been entitled to any compensation, and he was now on benefit. So far he hadn't been offered more work and the family was obviously struggling.

'She says to tell you, she's dreading winter,' the interpreter translated for Kelly. The older woman was embarrassed about her poor English and Carol had arranged a Samoan interpreter. Kelly had picked up a smattering of basic Samoan, Tongan and Maori over the years, but she was embarrassed about her own lack of knowledge. Each year she made a resolution to do something about improving her language skills, but she still hadn't found the time.

It seemed the home the family was renting was small and cramped and cold, and Tala had to share a tiny bedroom with three sisters.

Looking through the child's notes, Kelly saw that the rheumatic fever had damaged one of her heart valves, not enough, at this stage, to mean that surgical replacement was unavoidable, but it was important that she stayed in good health, had regular antibiotic injections and avoided any further infection.

'Things are looking stable,' she reassured Tala's mother once she'd finished examining her child. 'I see from the notes that our social worker has been trying to arrange a better house for you so that the children will have more room. Have you heard about that yet?'

The interpreter translated each answer with careful courtesy. 'She says Dr Jack has been talking to the social worker often and he has been writing letters to the department but they're still waiting to hear about a new house. She asks if he could try once more because she's worried about Tala getting sick again during the winter.'

'I'll talk to him,' Kelly promised. 'I'll talk to Dr Jack today and see if there's anything more we can do.'

'And she has brought some fruit,' the interpreter told her, after another brief exchange of communication. 'For Dr Jack, and for you of course, Dr Kelly.'

One of Tala's sisters had been sitting solemnly beside her mother, but she now came forward shyly with a large brown paper bag. Peeking inside, Kelly saw fresh feijoas. She inhaled the delicate floral fragrance of the small fruit. 'Thank you. They smell beautiful. I'll take some and give the rest to Dr Jack.'

She shook hands with Tala and her mother and sisters and the interpreter, and went with them to the door. By then Carol had Jack's next patient waiting for her in the other side room.

Kelly finished dictating her last letter for the session soon after seven. Spencer had gone but Jack was still working, she knew, because Carol had promised to tell him to check with her before he left. She gathered up her notes and the feijoas, tightened her nerves, straightened her shoulders, and went to find him.

He was alone in his office, dictating letters. He finished the one he was doing, then took out the tape and attached it to the top of the bundle of notes in front of him. 'All done,' he said heavily. 'Sorry I was away so long earlier. Thanks for covering.'

'No problem. How was the baby?'

'Small and flat and not wanting to breathe.' He grimaced. 'His mother's on methadone, and probably heroin as well, hence the concern. He came round after naloxone,' he said, referring to the antidote they used to reverse the effects of opiate drugs, 'but then he fitted.'

'Did you admit him to ICU?'

'That's why I was tied up so long,' he confirmed.

They discussed the baby then Kelly explained about seeing Tala. She gave him the feijoas. 'I said I'd ask you if you knew anything more about the housing situation.'

He looked tired. 'They still haven't heard about a move?'

'They haven't been told anything.'

'I'll try again tomorrow. I've lost count of the number of letters and phone calls I've made over this. The place is so badly ventilated that condensation drips from the walls and ceiling in winter. There's mould growing on the carpet in the bedrooms even now. It's not only Tala who's ill, both her sisters are asthmatic, and the youngest had pneumonia last year. I'll make more calls tomorrow. Something has to be done urgently or we're going to lose one of those kids.'

Kelly wished him well. She'd done battle for children on her own list living in similar conditions and she understood his frustration about nothing happening fast.

Jack collected the notes and the fruit. 'These smell great. Have you tried them?'

'I've kept a couple and I gave a few to Carol and the other nurses. Are you going to the wards?'

He nodded. 'I'll come up with you.

Although it hurt inside to look at Jack now, Kelly felt proud of herself for being able to hold a perfectly normal and professional conversation with him.

If you kept pretending you were sophisticated, she thought speculatively, then perhaps, eventually, you would be.

chapter fourteen

Most of the wards were full but because Roger's team had had a lot of admissions over the weekend his patients took up most of the beds, and Kelly's and Jack's loads were relatively low in comparison.

Tania had worked on the wards over the weekend because two staff nurses had been off sick, so she was off duty now and one of the other nurses accompanied them around their charges.

'Todd's weight is down,' she pointed out, when they visited the last of Jack's patients, a small boy with nephrotic syndrome, a problem where the kidneys grew leaky and let too much protein filter through into the urine. 'And his ankles don't look as swollen this morning.'

'The steroids are kicking in,' Jack murmured. Kelly took a hasty step back so that there was no risk of them touching as he moved past her to crouch beside the four-year-old's plastic chair at the main table. 'How's it going, cowboy?'

Todd, like the little girl he was colouring-in with, was dressed up in one of the ward's fringed leather jerkins and Stetsons, and Kelly smiled at their delighted grins at Jack's greeting. 'We're not cowboys,' Todd informed them, showing them the badge stuck to his top with Velcro, 'we're sheriffs.'

'My mistake.' Jack's lazy grin made Kelly's heart flutter in her chest. She watched while he swung his stethoscope from around his neck, lifted Todd's jerkin and pyjama top, and held the bell of the instrument just off the boy's back. 'How's it going, Sheriff?'

'Pretty good,' Todd assured him.

'Glad to hear it.' Jack listened to his chest and heart for a few moments and then examined his ankles and abdomen. 'We can start thinking about home now he's on the mend,' he declared when he rose from the children again. 'Tania, if his parents arrive while I'm still here tonight give me a call and I'll see how they feel about tomorrow. I'll need to follow him closely for now as an outpatient, weekly to start.'

'That'd be great.' The manager nodded. 'Thanks. We need as many beds as we can get right now.'

'You don't want a kidney biopsy?' Kelly asked.

They stopped at the notes trolley at the main desk and put the charts they'd been carrying into their alphabetical slots. 'Not if he keeps responding to the steroids,' Jack answered.

She nodded. Ninety per cent of the time, children in Todd's age group recovered normal kidney function with steroids, she knew. The decision to reserve biopsies for those children who failed to improve on standard treatment seemed a sensible one.

There was a stack of lab results on the desk where the ward clerk normally sat, and Kelly shuffled through the print-outs, for her own patients checking automatically that there were no abnormal results beyond the ones Spencer had already warned her about

'I forgot this.' Jack passed her a pen-torch. 'Emma, the drug rep earlier, had it for you.'

Emma. First names already. 'How kind.' Kelly took the torch from him then dumped it into the ward clerk's top drawer. 'Someone might find a use for it,' she added tightly. She already had a torch, and this one was decorated with the name of the company the woman had represented and the anti-histamine they were promoting.

'I warned her we wouldn't be recommending it be added to our prescribing list.'

'Thanks.' She sorted the results into consultant groups. 'They're mad thinking they can charge that much without offering a better product.' Ethically she disagreed with basing prescribing decisions on the cost of drugs, but there was no escaping the reality of the importance of competitive pricing in New Zealand's resource-strapped public health service. Here, at least, comparisons with other drugs made nonsense of this product's expense, so the decision not to use it didn't have to be a tortured one. 'Did she offer any explanation for the cost?'

'Didn't ask.' He changed X-rays. 'I didn't care.'

'I didn't get the impression she cared that much either. About the anti-histamine that is. Are you seeing her again?' It was out before she knew it and she bit her tongue, but it was too late to stop it, and when he looked up sharply, tea-green eyes narrowed, she had no choice but to brazen it out.

'*What?*'

'I'm curious.' She lowered her eyes to the results again, though she couldn't seem to focus on them. 'She seemed rather excitable. Or is it such an every-day thing for women to come on to you like that, that you don't notice it any more?'

'We must have been at different meetings.'

'Oh, come off it.' She slapped the results down. 'She virtually had her nipples exposed.'

He made an impatient sound. 'She was mildly flirtatious – '

'Any more mildly and she'd have been sitting on your face.'

She'd forgotten, in the emotion of the moment, that they were still on the ward, but strangled giggles behind brought her whirling around in shock. Two nurses who'd emerged from doing a dressing in the single room behind them had caught her comment. 'Oooh, Kelly,' Belinda, one of the more senior staff nurses on the ward, teased. 'That sounds interesting.' She grinned at Jack. 'Don't mind us.'

Kelly felt her face flame, all the more when Jack moved behind her and took her arm. He steered her towards the door. 'This feels like a good moment to leave. Goodnight, Sarah, Belinda.'

'Bye,' both women chimed behind them.

'I can't believe I said that,' Kelly murmured faintly, once they reached the relative safety of the corridor behind the main doors.

Jack shook his head as if he couldn't either. 'You did go overboard a bit.'

'I didn't mean I exaggerated,' she said sharply. She pulled away from him, irritated by the way her body had started to melt at being so close to him as much as by his bland denial that she hadn't seen what she had. 'I meant, I don't usually use such – graphic expressions. I'm in town tomorrow morning so I won't be out. Spencer knows all about everyone.'

'Wait!'

She wasn't far enough away by then to pretend that she hadn't heard so she stopped and turned round unwillingly but stayed where she was and let him catch up.

'Don't try to take the moral high ground around here, Sweetheart,' he warned, his voice low and gravely. 'You lost all right to that on Saturday night.'

'You pestered me for the truth about the money for weeks. It's not my fault you didn't like it when I gave it to you.' She felt her face flush hotly again. 'And I'm not your *sweetheart*. I realise it must be difficult keeping track of the names of all your women, considering the vast numbers there are of us, but since we work together I'd appreciate it if you tried harder to remember mine. And I didn't mention your morals, but then that may have been because you don't have any to mention.'

His face closed. 'She's a sales rep. It's her job to develop a rapport with us so that in future she can use that to sell us her company's products. You're overreacting. Nothing out of the normal happened there today.'

'I must have missed the bit where she established the rapport with me,' she retorted. 'And I must have missed the bit where she did that with Spencer. Because the funny thing is, all I saw was her fawning over you.'

'And that made you angry.'

'Of course it did.' She folded her arms. 'Naturally it did.' She faltered at the speculative light that came into his eyes then, and rushed on, 'I'm a busy person. My time is valuable and she wasted it.' She drew herself up to her full height. 'Just as you're wasting it now.'

His mouth tightened even further and his eyes turned hard. 'What do think happened? Do you think we – had sex – in the seminar room after you left?'

Only he didn't say *had sex*, he said something far more emotive and graphic, something that made Kelly recoil, and she mentally substituted the other phrase. 'I wouldn't be at all surprised,' she countered jerkily.

'Jealous?'

'You have to think that because your ego can't possibly

deal with the fact that I might simply have a valid complaint about her professionalism.'

'She was professional enough.' He took a step towards her. 'Unlike you right now. Is this going to happen every time some woman looks at me?'

'I hope not,' she burst out. 'I'd be insane by Easter.'

'You have no right to be jealous.' He slapped both hands hard against the wall, startling her into starting to back away. 'You gave away any right to that.'

'Unfortunately I'm not as profoundly insensitive as you,' she retorted. 'I'm not as experienced as you obviously are at jumping into bed with someone, then tossing them unfeelingly out of my home the next day. But I dare say with a bit more practice – '

'Firstly, there was nothing,' he said between gritted teeth, '*unfeeling* about it. Secondly, as a woman who calmly tells a man she wants to sleep with him so she can fantasise about being in bed with her mongrel of an ex-husband, I believe we can take it as read that you're running a distant last in the sensitivity race. Thirdly... '

But Kelly was still stuck on number two. 'That's why you were angry coming back from the party? Because you thought I was going to be thinking of Warwick?'

'It's the sort of thing that grates on a man's nerves... '

'But I didn't. That's not what I meant. Of course I wouldn't be thinking of him. I've spent years going out of my way not to.' She was shocked. 'I thought you were disgusted because I told you I still slept with him when he had other women. I thought you were put you off that I could be so – unrefined – '

'There's nothing unrefined about a healthy enjoyment of sex,' he interjected tersely. 'If it was good with him, I'm glad for you. I might not want to think too much about it, but if he pleased you that way then terrific. He sure as hell didn't do you any other favours.'

'But you looked shocked. I thought you had this delicate image of me in your head and you were cross that I didn't fit it any more.'

'Delicate? I don't expect you to be delicate. I don't expect you to be anything but what you are. Nothing you could tell me would shock me. Nothing would change the way I feel about you. And if you'd shown a fraction more sensitivity to my feelings Sunday – '

'If *I'd* shown more sensitivity! All I said to you was that you remind me of Warwick. And you do. I didn't say anything about this fantasy stuff, that's straight out of your head. You're the one who threw me out on Sunday. You're the one carrying on with drug reps right in front of me. You're the one driving around in a car that I can't even look at any more without seeing pictures in my head of all the women you've had in there. You're the one who doesn't have any idea how hard this is for me working alongside you here surrounded by your – conquests. Everywhere I look I see another one. How do you imagine that makes me feel?'

'Deluded?' he offered. 'Paranoid?'

'It's not me who has the mental problem,' she retorted violently. 'It's not me who has to have it off with every available partner to prove heaven-knows-what to myself. Just out of curiosity, is there any woman on Maui you haven't seen naked yet?'

'Just out of curiosity, do you really think you can use me as a sick way of reminding yourself of your ex-husband, yet still think you're fit to stand in judgement on the way I lead my life?'

'I told you,' she cried. 'I didn't do that.'

'And what does any of this have to do with the Porsche – '

'Veronica!' she snapped curtly.

He gave a heavy sigh and she nodded grimly.

'Veronica – the MD's personal assistant. Maybe you really didn't make love to her in the Porsche – and maybe you did. Who knows? But just thinking about you and that "passion wagon" of yours makes me feel ill!'

Her comments disturbed him, she could tell from the way he ran his hand jerkily through his hair. He leaned against the metal hand rail along the corridor wall. 'Veronica is just a black widow spider. I've already told you that nothing happened. But it didn't stop you wanting sex with me, did it?'

'Because I didn't understand,' she countered. 'I didn't understand how it was with you. I didn't understand how it would be. I expected it to be more – urgent,' she went on hoarsely, when he simply waited, silent, for her to continue. 'Less touching. I thought it would be fast. Passionate. Great, really great, but unemotional, the way it was going to be the last time after the beach. Right up until we made love I thought I was going to be able to get up afterwards and be perfectly fine and I thought I'd be able to carry on as if it had never happened.'

'But that's what you did.'

'Only because you forced me to.' Her legs trembling, she sank on to the opposite rail. 'I could hardly think, but you didn't give me any choice about leaving. At the moment it still hurts me to think of you being with other women the way you were with me. I know that's stupid. I know it's just like having a cake and wanting to eat it too but I can't help myself. It hurts to think of you sharing that sort of intimacy with Veronica and those other women. I didn't mean to feel this way, and I don't want to, and I'm sorry that I do, but it's just a fact. It's probably why I overreacted so badly about that rep today. I'm sorry. You're right, I have no right to be jealous. Your – social life is none of my business.'

'You don't think, Kelly. Not when you're with me. You react on instinct. In your head I'm your ex-husband all over again. You make assumptions without facts. Consciously or not, you're still determined to punish me for him. He played around on you, so you're convinced I will. I'm no monk, I won't pretend that. But I'm interested in you now, not Veronica, not Donna Ling, not anyone else but you.'

Kelly felt weak. 'So what happened with us was special for you? Not A for mediocre?'

'More even than D for extraordinary,' he said roughly. 'Make it Z, for out of this world.'

She pushed her legs out in front of her, slipped her shoes off, and studied her feet again. 'Well, we agree on something at least.' She pushed her feet back into her shoes again quickly and levered herself away from the rail.

'The difference is that we made love.' He rose slowly opposite her. 'That wasn't sex, it was love. You may be determined beyond reason to go on ignoring it, but that was the difference.'

'I know. I recognised that.' Their eyes met and clung and she felt a thin shaft of pain shoot through her chest. The irony, she knew, was exquisitely poignant. 'Why me?'

He made a small, almost indifferent shrugging movement with one shoulder. 'I can tell you why I'm attracted to you, but that wouldn't give the whole answer. You said it yourself, you don't choose. It happens.'

'I said, you don't *always* choose. A person should have some choice. He or she should be able to keep from doing something utterly stupid. This shouldn't have happened. It's madness that it has. With everything I know about living with a man like you I should have been immune to you,' she continued weakly. 'Being with Warwick should have been like being vaccinated. Perhaps I'm a masochist?'

'Stop blaming me for him.'

She gathered her bag against herself, defensive against the cold, angry darkening of his eyes. 'If it helps your pride recover faster, you're better. Way, way better. He isn't even anywhere near your league. But plenty of other things are the same. Just out of interest, if you ever marry how long do you think you'll be able to stay faithful?'

'In my world marriage vows are sacred.'

She smiled thinly. 'Warwick used to reassure me too. And after every lapse, he'd promise he was reformed. But it was never true. With him that used to hurt. With you, I have a feeling it might kill me.'

She felt his fury at that like a fire around her but he didn't move. He simply folded his arms and eyed her coolly. 'I know I could push you. I know I could persuade you. I could use sex or I could use everything else I have to force you to see and to believe me, Kelly. But I'm not going to because every couple goes through hard times at some stage and unless the change comes from within you, all that pushing you would do, would be to give you an excuse to back out further down the line. It's up to you. You have to make the decision to trust me and if you can't do that then I'm walking away.'

'I understand.' She already knew what her decision was, what it *had* to be. She knew what the right thing for herself was, and she knew that when she turned away from him now, he'd understand her too.

She started away, took a few steps, but then stopped and turned round slowly. His face had closed to her, but she spoke anyway. 'What was the third thing?'

At his uncomprehending look she went on, 'Before. You said there were three things. One, you weren't unfeeling. Two, you said I was the least sensitive one. You didn't finish the third.'

He closed his eyes briefly. 'Three, you said something about needing more practice at walking away the morning after, and my response was going to be that you might as well forget about that, because you're not going to get any more practice.'

'I see.' She swallowed heavily. That was her option then. She either gave him everything he thought he wanted, or there'd never be anything – there was no middle way. No casual arrangement would be permitted. Which meant that now was the end of everything. She would have to leave Karori, of course – as soon as she had her debts paid off. She couldn't stand by and watch him with other women the way he'd always be with them. But losing a job would be vastly less traumatic than losing her mind.

She was on call Thursday, then frantic on Friday morning, then busy with her private clinic until late. At the weekend she covered a friend's general practice in Wellington, and she was at the main hospital for her oncology clinic on Monday. It was late in the afternoon before she drove to Karori for her night on call.

Jack had filled her thoughts for the four days she hadn't seen him, but he must have already left for the evening because he wasn't around when she made it to the hospital.

She was torn between relief at not having to face him and desolation that it was so long since she'd had her last fix of him. Knowing that it was over, and knowing that in a year's time, when she was free of her financial responsibilities, she was going to have to leave the hospital and probably Wellington as well, wasn't helping break her addiction. Yet it seemed she was going to have to wait yet another day.

Spencer was on Maui ward waiting to go around with her. Tania and Roger were at the desk close to him, ostensibly going through the admissions book.

'I couldn't believe it when I heard,' Tania was saying dismally to Roger when Kelly came up to them.

'I wish he'd warned me.' Roger looked equally gloomy.

'He has to be mad,' Spencer contributed.

'Who's mad, and you wish who'd warned you what, Roger?' Kelly asked, as she came up. 'What am I missing out on?'

Tania turned with a sad look. 'Jack sold the Porsche at the weekend.'

Kelly went cold. *'What?'*

'He's bought a four-wheel-drive like mine,' Roger said miserably. 'No more weekend jaunts for me while he goes surfing.'

'He says it's more practical,' Tania added. 'We can't believe it.'

They said other things, over her head, but Kelly hardly heard any of it because her brain was too distracted by the sudden pounding of her blood in her ears.

'But it was brand new,' she protested faintly, interrupting after a little while. 'He must have lost thousands on it.' She paled at the thought of the price he'd probably paid for it. 'Tens of thousands even.'

'It doesn't make sense,' said Spencer. 'Who in their right mind would give up a car like that *and* sell it at the worst time for taking a huge depreciation loss?'

Kelly felt almost sick. She looked vaguely at Spencer. 'Can we go on the round, please?' She had to focus on work while she was here and she needed to familiarise herself again with the wards. And then she had to find Jack. She had to find him immediately.

It was still daylight when they finished – February still had long days, and the end of daylight saving, when the evenings suddenly drew in darkly, seemed like a long way away – but a gale warning had been issued for overnight and the air was cool now. It was already windy enough to loosen strands from her topknot and send them flying around her face.

She crossed her arms to keep out the chill and hurried directly over to Jack's, her bleep and the hospital mobile phone safely in her bag in case Spencer needed to contact her. She wasn't even sure what she was going to say to Jack, but after hearing about the car she knew she couldn't wait until the next day to see him.

But there was no reply when she rang the bell, and the space where he normally parked was empty.

Jack's neighbour, a surgeon at the hospital, came out from next door carrying a rubbish bag. 'Kelly, hi!' he called, lifting his arm in a wave as he headed for the bins lined up for collection. 'Jack said something about going to Lyall Bay. He had a couple of boards with him. There's good wave sailing there in a southerly.'

'I'll come back later,' she called back. She stepped off the porch and looked doubtfully at the weather. Conditions at the beach would be blustery and unpleasant, and she decided Jack wouldn't be long.

But she thought about that again and realised he'd relish conditions that repelled saner, more sensible people, and so she diverted to the car park and collected her car. There were several surfers in the water at Lyall Bay, two on big boards and the rest on small ones. One other man was on shore, just off the road, but he was packing up, and when Kelly walked on to the beach she heard him talking into a mobile phone and saying the conditions were too rough for him.

She shielded her eyes from the wind and looked out anxiously towards Jack. The big seas made even him look small, and she caught her breath with a mixture of fear and exhilaration as he turned the board expertly, then headed fast back across the bay towards the shore, the board surging and leaping, lifting above the waves as the wind filled the sail.

Kelly felt precisely the moment he saw her. He was still beyond the crashing breakers and too far off shore for her to make out his features, but she felt her body's instinctive physical response to his eyes locking on hers. She saw the board stop suddenly as the sail twisted and lost wind, and as if her being there had thrown him off balance, for the first time ever she saw him lose control of the board. She gasped when another wave caught the board, bucked it like a horse and threw him into the water.

She went up on to her toes anxiously, but his dark head appeared from under the water almost immediately, and as she watched he gripped the board and held on to it, controlling it through the next heavy swells, obviously waiting for the water to calm a little before he attempted to climb back on.

Fingers trembling, Kelly opened her mobile. Roger had told her he'd be staying late, and when he answered his office phone she asked him if he could cover her for an hour.

'Sure.' He sounded unconcerned. 'Take all you want. I owe you big time still anyway. Spencer's with me now and I'll let switchboard know. What's up?'

She stared at the waves and tried not to be frightened. 'I'm going,' she said shakily, 'for a swim.'

chapter fifteen

Kelly left her phone and bleep with her clothes in her car. The surfers were too busy coping with the conditions to take any notice of her and there'd be no spectators in conditions like this. Even if people in passing cars saw her, her bra and panties were modestly cut and black and sort of matching, and she figured they'd pass for a bikini.

Considering Jack had stroked and kissed and praised every centimetre of her, all the bits both outside and inside her underwear, she didn't expect he'd die of shock either.

He'd climbed on the board now but he just lay across it, making no attempt to come in, watching her as she walked down to the water.

The spray stung her skin with every blast of wind. She steeled herself for ice, but the water was warmer than she'd expected, and after the cold, wind-chilled air it was almost a relief to submerge herself in it. Keeping well clear of the rocks and with her head low to avoid the worst of the wind and spray, she paddled out through the terrifying breakers.

He laughed as she came up to him. He caught her around the waist and helped her on to the board, supporting her with his wet suit-covered body so that she didn't slide off again as they rolled up and over the next wave.

'You are an extraordinary woman,' he shouted against her ear so that she could hear him over the wind and the surf, as his hands released the clips from her hair and sent it tumbling into damp, disordered chaos around them.

'It's not so bad.' She tossed her hair away from her face and over her back, and looked over her shoulder and laughed at him. 'Now I'm here it's not as frightening as I expected it to be. I must be getting a taste for excitement.'

'About time.' He put her clips into the pocket of his suit, then caught a handful of her flying hair between his fingers and held it briefly to his face. 'Up to a ride?'

'Won't we sink?'

'Probably.' But he laughed. 'Worth a try.'

'You're mad,' she shouted back. 'Just don't expect me to stay on more than ten seconds.'

'You'll stay on.' He released her hair, helped her up to a crouch, then came up behind her, lifting the sail in a single, smooth motion. 'Hold there,' he ordered, guiding her hands to the horizontal beam.' He wasn't wearing a harness, she realised. 'Lean hard into me. We have to be one rider.'

It was exhilarating. Once she'd have been too frightened to contemplate being this far out in even calm weather, but suddenly, surrounded by storm, she felt free and wild and eager, and instead of worrying she laughed. They went out fast, flying like the wind itself, then she pushed herself tight against him, following his shouted instructions so that they turned as one and came racing back in towards the beach without falling off.

They did it once more, out and back, then he let her off into the water and dropped the sail. 'The wind's shifting,' he shouted, waving for her to swim ahead of him. 'Go in, I'll come behind you.'

The wind caught at the sail, flinging it about when he dragged it up away from the water, and they had to work fast together to control it and get it protected.

The surfers had gone now and it was growing dark. While Jack finished packing the board and sail into their zipper bags, Kelly tipped forward and squeezed as much water as she could out of her hair. She quickly retrieved her clothes from the car, crouched behind it and shed her wet underwear, mopped at her skin with her shirt, then hauled on her jeans and jersey directly against her shivering skin.

Her feet still bare, she straightened at the crash of a particularly violent wave. Shielding her eyes from the wind and flying spray, she stared out at where they'd been. 'How dangerous was that?'

'Not much,' Jack shouted back. 'You could have drowned, but you wouldn't have been swept out.' He made a careless gesture. 'Tide's coming in and the wind's coming south-east now, driving us on shore. Why?' He finished hauling up the board's zipper and rose from his crouch with a grin. 'Think you're a daredevil now?'

'There's a radical idea. Maybe I am. Teach me to surf?'

He sent her a surprised look. 'Do you mean that?'

'Why not?' She shrugged. 'If I could go out in that tonight, I should manage to stand on a board on its own when it's calm.'

'If you're so brave suddenly, say you'll come flying with me.'

'I've told you before,' she shouted, when the wind lifted again, 'only if you promise me we'll join the mile high club.'

'No.' He flung her a distracted look, finished packing the board, then left it and came over to her. He was broad and powerful-looking in his wet suit, and her body ached looking at him. 'It's never worth the hype.'

As of course he had to know. She jerked her head back

and slapped at his arm with the back of her hand, but he took her face in his hands and kissed her hard. When he lifted his head she stared up at him, her heart beating so fast that she could feel it through her whole body.

'Good girl.'

'I look at you and my head spins,' she whispered.

'Then it's time to fly.' His hands slid from her face, over the aching curve of her breasts and lower to her hips. He held her hard and his strength turned her dizzy. 'You mean the world to me, Kelly. I'm not your ex-husband. I will never hurt you.'

She wanted to believe him. She ached to believe him. 'I love you. More than I ever realised it was possible to love. That's what you want to hear, isn't it?'

'It's a start.' But he didn't smile. 'I want everything. Give it to me. You braved the storm, you walked trembling into the water and you swam to me. I can't be so frightening after that.'

'In the water I could only drown. You scare me much more than that.'

'You don't think you do the same to me?' He brushed her wet hair back from her face. 'The way I feel about you scares the hell out of me. It has done since the start. Until I saw you walking towards me tonight, I was starting to think you might not ever be brave enough to give me what I want. But now I know you can handle it, I won't accept any compromise. Nothing's changed, Kelly. Either you give me everything, or we have nothing.'

'You *can* have all of me.' She ached for him to kiss her again. 'You know you can. Any time. Anywhere. I promise.'

'Uh, uh, Sweetheart.' Instead of deepening their embrace the way she craved, he released her. 'You're going to have to do a lot better than that.'

While he collected the board and the sail, she fetched her watch from her car and trailed after him, carrying her underwear and her shirt, the phone and the bleep.

'I didn't think a man could be this unselfish,' she said quietly, watching him strap the windsurfer on to the roof rack atop a gleaming, silver four-wheel-drive. 'I didn't think it was possible. I am utterly incredulous that you did this.'

'Is that why you're here?' He stilled. *'Because I sold the Porsche?'*

'You did it for me, didn't you?'

'Not to prove anything.' He looked puzzled. 'I wasn't making a grand gesture. Anyway,' he lifted his arms, 'there were plenty of reasons for getting rid of it apart from you hating it.'

She smiled. She looked down at her trainers and kicked a pebble. 'Oh, yeah?'

'No room for my boards. No remote central locking. I was sick of Roger pestering me every weekend to borrow it.'

'Mmm, all reasonable grounds for sacrificing the car of your dreams,' she mused.

'If you miss it too much, we can buy another one with the money we're going to force out of your ex.'

She glanced up in time to catch the narrowed look he sent her, before he turned back to loading the windsurfer. 'If I'd known selling the Porsche would have this effect on you, I'd have done it weeks ago.'

Her face warmed. She let the comment about Warwick go. It seemed trivial besides what she was about to say. 'The car had to go eventually. We'd never have been able to fit kids in it.'

She saw him stiffen momentarily. He tightened the last of the straps in hard, fast movements, then came around to where she stood. '*What*?'

'Not yet,' she said quickly. 'I'm not pregnant,' she assured him. He'd been careful of that. 'But I've been thinking perhaps I should take your advice and talk to an obstetrician. Next week, I thought. I think I should hear what advice he can give me. Just in case he thinks there's a chance.'

'I'll come with you.' He put his arms around her. 'If it doesn't happen, it doesn't happen, and I'll be happy with that because you matter more to me than anything else in this world, but it's worth a try.'

'If it doesn't work, I'd like to consider fostering.' He'd peeled his wet suit to his waist and she buried her face against his damp chest. 'Would that be all right?'

'Anything's all right.' His hands stroked her back. 'As long as I have you.' The wind was drying her hair fast and it blew up around her head. He caught it and smoothed it down over her shoulders. 'You should know, I wanted you with me last weekend. I'm telling you now because I don't want any more secrets between us. There was no double-booking with your job. I paid them enough to get someone else so that you'd have the time free.'

She lifted her head. 'Just so that I would spend the day with you?'

'I was sick of waiting for you to come around to my way of thinking. It felt like time to force things along.'

'You are a shameless manipulator,' she accused.

'Not all the time, but with that, yes. I warned you weeks ago how much I wanted you, so you should have known I wouldn't give up at simple hurdles.'

'I should be angry.'

'Are you?'

'I don't know.' She shook her head, uncertain. 'I don't think so. I think I might be – flattered. That was a lot of trouble to go to to teach me to windsurf.'

He smiled. 'Mostly I wanted to see you in a wet suit.'

Remembering what had happened when he had, she felt herself flush hotly again. 'I have to call Roger.' She put her clothes under her arm and opened her phone. 'He's been covering me. I have to tell him I'm taking over again.'

But when she punched out the numbers, Jack took the phone from her. He fended her off with one hand when she tried to get it back. 'Stop delaying,' he told her roughly. 'Putting me off won't make me go away and I want everything set in stone with you. Roger?' he went on, talking into the phone. 'Jack. Listen, Kelly's staying with me tonight. It's kind of a big night for us. You couldn't – you could? Great. Yep. Thanks, mate. Appreciate it. I owe you one.'

He lifted the phone away from her frustrated attempts to wrench it from him, and put it on top of his roof rack, out of her reach unless she managed to get past him first.

'That's any hope of privacy ruined,' she accused. 'Roger will tell everyone – '

'I hope so.' But his shrug was nonchalant and he controlled her struggles easily by simply turning her round and dragging her back against him. He retrieved a towel from the back of the wagon and took a few seconds to turban it around her wet hair. 'Self-protection,' he claimed against her ear. He massaged her scalp through the towel. 'Tania's threatened to break my legs if I hurt you. This way at least she'll know as fast as possible that I've tried to do the right thing.'

'I'll break both your legs if you don't let me go,' she threatened violently, but her kicks were ineffectual against his strength, and she knew from his soft laughter as he used the excuse of containing her to let his hands explore under her clothes, that he knew it too.

'You're cold,' he murmured, when her struggles ceased and she shivered against him. 'I shouldn't have kept you out.' He opened the door and pushed her inside. 'I'll take you home and we'll pick up your car tomorrow. You need to get your hair dry and you need a hot shower.'

'And you need a cold one,' she retorted meaningfully, clutching at the towel around her hair when it threatened to unwind, and glaring at him when he read her mind and scooped the phone easily out of reach before she could grab it again.

She wound down her window and watched hungrily as he shed his wet suit and pulled on thigh-hugging jeans and a thick jersey. Then he climbed in beside her, put another towel around her shoulders, and started the engine.

'You do realise I won't let you conceive my child out of wedlock,' he said conversationally.

'That's very old-fashioned of you.'

His mouth hardened, but the swift, hungry look he sent her promised retribution for that. 'Wedding or nothing, Kelly. I've been waiting for you all my life and you're the only woman I want. Nothing will ever be more important to me than your happiness. I know your life hasn't been easy until now, I understand why you're wary, but it's time to move on.'

'I do trust you, you know.' She looked out of her window. 'When I heard about you selling the car – well, I accept that my memories of Warwick have biased me against you.' She smiled a little. Her ex-husband would have sold *her* to a car dealer if he'd thought it'd give him a discount on a Porsche.

She said, 'But you're very desirable. Even without the past to bias me I would always have found it hard to believe you'd choose to give up other women just for me.'

'Believe me, I recognised the irony of that fairly early on,' he said gravely. 'Kelly, to me you're the most lovely, desirable woman in the world. You've driven me half-way to hell and back at times, but I haven't looked at anyone else since the day I met you and I never will.'

Kelly swallowed hard. 'What about Donna Ling?'

'Donna?' He looked confused. 'Nothing happened there.'

'So you didn't sleep with her the night we went to Makara? The night you took her to the golf club.'

'I didn't take her, she turned up. I didn't know she was going to be there. I didn't touch her.' He clamped his hands over the steering wheel, his expression bemused. 'The only woman on my mind that night was you. Hell, Kelly, get over this. You have no reason to be insecure. You're the only woman on my mind every night. And you're the only woman I've ever asked to marry me.'

She smiled. 'You just can't handle the sex object thing.'

He glanced at her, then steered the car off the kerb and on to the road, driving towards the city. 'I'm more than happy to be your sex object. I just need a wedding ring for security first.'

Security? Jack? She looked at him sharply. He couldn't be nervous...could he? Not of her. 'You're bossy and demanding and you scare me when you do dangerous things, but you're still a warm, kind, wonderful man and I do love you, Jack, I promise. '

'Yep.' He didn't look at her. 'So you said.'

But he didn't sound convinced. She looked away. He'd turned up the heat, and although her extremities remained cold she felt warmth slowly beginning to creep back into her chest. Compared with the Porsche and her own car she felt high up and she could see right over the fences they were passing, into the living rooms of the houses beyond.

'You can't talk,' she murmured after a little while. 'You haven't once said you love me.'

'No, I'm driving a tank for the joy of it.'

She looked at him sharply again but he seemed to be concentrating on driving. Preoccupied with her own thoughts, she was silent for the rest of the drive.

He didn't turn off at her flat but drove straight up to Karori. He turned into the grounds of the hospital, slowed opposite the townhouse and attempted a U turn. He made a harsh sound when the four-wheel-drive failed to make it in one, forcing him to throw it into reverse. He saw her smile and sent her a menacing look as he lurched it forward again into a parking space. 'How dare you doubt me,' he growled.

They went into the house. Jack put the back of his hands against her cold face and hands as if checking her temperature, then propelled her upstairs, thrust thick, clean towels into her arms, and turned on the shower for her. 'I'll put soup on to heat,' he told her, withdrawing with slow, intoxicating reluctance as she started to undress. 'Take your time,' he added huskily. 'Make sure you get properly warm.'

The heated water was wonderful against her chilled flesh and she lingered ages under it, using his shampoo to soap the salt and sand out of her hair. Her clothes were damp so she wrapped her hair in a dry towel, wrapped another around her hips, and went into Jack's bedroom and chose a neatly folded T-shirt from a pile of fresh washing on his dresser.

Jack had made toast and warmed tomato soup for her, and she ate the meal hungrily while he showered. 'I like this.' His hands slid beneath the T-shirt appreciatively when he returned while she was rinsing the dishes. 'And this.' He released the towel holding her hair and she felt the damp weight tumbling down her back. 'I love this.' She felt him nuzzling the back of her head. 'I could drown in your hair. I love you, Kelly. I love everything about you. Now tell me properly that you've fallen in love with me.'

Kelly arched against him, her skin melting beneath the slow slide of his hands across her midriff. 'I've properly fallen in love with you.'

'Too fast.' His hands cupped her breasts and flattened them fractionally. 'Tell me seriously.'

She tipped her head forward. 'Seriously,' she said slowly. 'I didn't mean it and I didn't want it to happen, and part of me still thinks it's a disaster that it has, but you have brought an excitement to my life I never dreamed I'd experience and I have fallen in love with you.'

'Disaster? Hmm. That's not a nice thing to say.' But his hands grew tender. 'I'll let it pass this time. Tell me your life is worthless without me.'

'Worthless,' she agreed mournfully.

His hands crossed over, cupped her opposite breasts, and he lifted her back against him, the knot of the towel at his hips rough against her buttocks. 'You accused me once of having something missing in my life,' he muttered. 'You were right. I realised that day, that what I was missing was you. Now I want a wedding. Big, small, I don't care. I want to meet your Mum and your sister and her family, and I want them to come and stay with us so that we can all get to know each other right away. It's time.'

'You're not going to give up on this one, hmm?'

'Never.' He laughed. 'It's right, Kelly. Nothing in my life has ever felt so right as this. I want to spend the rest of my life with you, so why muck around? Let's just do it. Be brave, my darling.'

'If I said no, would I lose you?'

'No, now I've got you this far that would be my cue to begin playing with you till you were so mindlessly aroused you'd say anything I wanted.'

'Oh, I like the sound of that.' She reached up and kissed him lingeringly then drew back slowly. 'OK, we'll get married and then I might as well come flying and learn rock-climbing and travel with you because nothing else will ever feel more dangerous.'

'You're such a wimp,' he accused roughly. 'You don't understand yet that saying yes is infinitely safer for you, my love, than saying no. I make you complete, the same way you complete me. If you turn me down I'll have to spend the rest of my life pestering you to change your mind.'

'I think I'll take up sky-diving.'

'Then maybe a round-the-world yacht race would be fun,' he agreed, getting rid of her towel.

'Scuba diving,' she added cheerfully. 'White water rafting. Canoeing.'

He laughed against her throat. 'That's the honeymoon taken care of,' he taunted. He slid the T-shirt over her head. 'Then when we get back I'll teach you about real adventure.'

'Mountaineering,' she offered hoarsely. 'You're going to drag me up Mount Cook.'

'The real adventure's going to be exploring you,' he murmured, lifting her in his arms and carrying her effortlessly up the stairs. 'It's going to last for the rest of our lives. Are you ready for that one, Kelly?'

She kissed him. 'I guess once the honeymoon's out of the way that won't feel so scary.'

He laughed. He tumbled her down on to the bed and she closed her eyes. It felt for a second as if she were jumping though space, but then he came over her and caught her, and when she opened her eyes she was in his arms.

Kelly smiled. She looked up, into his face, and touched him. She realised that beyond the desire and the wanting and the craving she needed him to satisfy, she suddenly felt utterly and completely secure. 'I love you,' she whispered. 'But I still can't believe you sold the Porsche.'

'I seem to have snared the tank and the girl.' He cupped her breasts. 'I figure I'm up on the deal.'

'You must really love the tank,' she teased.

'Hate the tank.' He lowered his mouth to hers and kissed her, and when he lifted his head he smiled and touched her mouth wonderingly with his fingers.

'But I'm crazy,' he said softly, 'absolutely crazy about the girl.'

Romance at its best from Heartline Books™

We're that sure you've enjoyed the latest selection of titles from Heartline. We can offer you even more new novels by our talented authors over the coming months. Heartline will be bringing you stories with a dash of mystery, some which are tinged with humour and others highlighting the passion and pain of love lost and re-discovered. Our unique and eye-catching covers will capture backdrops which include the glamorous, exotic desert, an idyllic watermill in the English countryside and the charm of a traditional bookshop.

Whatever the setting, you can be sure that our heroes and heroines will be people you will care about and want to spend time with. Authors we shall be featuring will include Angela Drake, Harriet Wilson and Clare Tyler, while each month we will do our best to bring you an author making her sparkling debut in the world of romantic fiction.

If you've enjoyed these books why not tell all your friends and relatives that they, too, can start a new romance with Heartline Books today, by applying for their own, **ABSOLUTELY FREE**, copy of Natalie Fox's LOVE IS FOREVER. To obtain their free book, they can:

- visit our website: www.heartlinebooks.com
- *or* telephone the Heartline Hotline on 0845 6000504
- *or* enter their details on the form below, tear it off and send it to:
  Heartline Books,
  FREEPOST LON 16243, Swindon, SN2 8LA

And, like you, they can discover the joys of subscribing to Heartline Books, including:

- ♥ A wide range of quality romantic fiction delivered to their door each month
- ♥ A monthly newsletter packed with special offers, competitions, celebrity interviews and other exciting features
- ♥ A bright, fresh, new website created just for our readers

Heartline Books...

Romance at its best™

Please send me my free copy of *Love is Forever*:

Name (IN BLOCK CAPITALS) .

_____

Address (IN BLOCK CAPITALS)

_____

_____

_____

_____ Postcode _____

If you do not wish to receive selected offers
from other companies, please tick the box   ☐

If we do not hear from you within the next ten days, we will be sending you four exciting new romantic novels at a price of £3.99 each, plus £1 p&p. Thereafter, each time you buy our books, we will send you a further pack of four titles.